The pressure of his hands on hers as they guided Sundance *through the narrow channel between the headlands felt sure and solid.*

She turned her head, looked up at him and smiled, loving the way his eyes crinkled at the corners, the way the corners of his mouth lifted, as he smiled back.

The water in the cove was quiet and calm, the low sun sending golden shafts of light across the aquamarine sea. Jensen cut the engine so that the only sound was the lap of the ripples against the hull and then the splash of the anchor.

Beth didn't want to move. She wanted to hold on to this moment for as long as possible, the warmth of Jensen's body pressed against the length of her back and thighs, the feel of his steady breath brushing against her cheek. He lifted her hands from the wheel, folding them in his. Her breathing became shallow, her heartbeat loud in her ears.

Dear Reader,

Beth's stepmother and stepsister have ruled her life, but when she's free of them, unemployed and homeless, the future feels alien and frightening. An isolated villa on the Turkish Turquoise Coast provides the solitude she needs to plan a new life.

Jensen Heath, released from prison after a miscarriage of justice, has one aim: to sail his ketch, *Sundance*, to the Turkish cove he once visited years before. There he believes he will find the peace he needs to heal.

Both Beth and Jensen are incensed to find they must share the beach and sheltered bay they each regard as their own.

But soon their mutual distrust becomes a wary friendship. Might this be the opportunity for romance that has always passed Beth by, and the chance for Jensen to rebuild his trust in life and love?

Must they each tread a lonely path into the future, or will they find a way to navigate the difficult times ahead together?

The idyllic Turquoise Coast and the intriguing ruins of the sunken city of Kekova were the inspiration for Beth and Jensen's story. I hope you will enjoy reading it.

Suzanne

CINDERELLA'S ADVENTURE WITH THE CEO

SUZANNE MERCHANT

ROMANCE

Harlequin®
ROMANCE

ISBN-13: 978-1-335-21608-3

Cinderella's Adventure with the CEO

Harlequin Enterprises ULC
22 Adelaide St. West, 41st Floor
Toronto, Ontario M5H 4E3, Canada
www.Harlequin.com

Printed in U.S.A.

Recycling programs for this product may not exist in your area.

Suzanne Merchant was born and raised in South Africa. She and her husband lived and worked in Cape Town, London, Kuwait, Baghdad, Sydney and Dubai before settling in the Sussex countryside. They enjoy visits from their three grown-up children and are kept busy attempting to wrangle two spaniels, a dachshund, a parrot and a large, unruly garden under control.

Books by Suzanne Merchant

Harlequin Romance

Their Wildest Safari Dream
Off-Limits Fling with the Billionaire
Ballerina and the Greek Billionaire
Heiress's Escape to South Africa

Visit the Author Profile page at Harlequin.com.

For Saffet and the staff of the pansiyon at Simena
who welcome their guests with unfailing
warmth and hospitality.

Praise for
Suzanne Merchant

"This is an intensely emotional and immensely
satisfying read. With a few well-chosen words the
author takes the reader to the heart of the African
bush and into the hearts of her protagonists.
I thoroughly recommend it."

—Amazon customer on *Their Wildest Safari Dream*

CHAPTER ONE

No ONE KNEW where Jensen Heath had gone. And that was exactly how he wanted it. Five weeks earlier, when he'd walked through the prison gates a free man, declared the victim of a miscarriage of justice, he'd contacted nobody. Returning to his city penthouse, he'd stood at the wide glass windows and studied the view. A new building had altered the skyline in the past year, but far below, the grey ribbon of the Thames had continued to wind its timeless path towards the sea. The vista was virtually unchanged, and yet to him it would never be the same again. He'd become a different man, one who viewed the world through a lens distorted by anger and bitterness.

He'd turned away, packed a cabin bag with a few essentials and called the concierge, asking for a taxi to Heathrow.

The rattle of the chain and then the splash of the anchor hitting the water sounded thunderous, disturbing the still of the night. Jensen returned to the wheel in the cockpit and shifted the gears into neutral, allowing *Sundance* to drift astern until the metal spikes dug into the seabed and tugged her to a gentle stop. The throb of the engine, a muffled counterpoint to the soft wash of the sea on the beach, died away as he hit the 'off' button.

Jensen exhaled into the almost-silence, listening for anything out of place. An owl hooted somewhere in the belt of trees behind the beach, and the water, which he knew would be like warm silk on his skin, lapped at the hull. He was tempted to slip over the side for a swim but chose instead to simply absorb the atmosphere.

This was the place he'd dreamed of when the nights had been disturbed by the clang of a metal cell door, the snapping shut of a grille, voices raised in argument somewhere nearby. It felt miraculous that he'd found his way back, sailing solo from Piraeus in Greece; that he'd plotted his course to bring his boat to the narrow entrance between two embracing headlands on the Turkish coast, and then slipped her through the gap, into the cove he'd come to think of as belonging to him.

Managing the forty-foot ketch on his own had been a challenge, at times. Some of the sailing had been hard, and the way he'd pushed the boat to her limits had taken its toll, not just on the boat but on his body, too. Yet he'd relished the days when the wind and weather had demanded his full attention, leaving no room for the memories of his unjust incarceration, and the anger they stirred up, at times when he had space to think.

He stood and stretched, aware of the slight stiffness that had crept into his muscles and joints over the past few weeks. An old injury made his left shoulder ache. Twenty-five years ago, shouting the odds on the trading floor, he'd been supple and strong, working hard all hours of the day and playing even harder in the few left at night. Success and wealth had allowed him to slow down a little. And yes, he admitted wryly to himself, age had played its part.

He tidied the cockpit and then dragged his thin, rolled-up mattress from the locker on the foredeck. Stretching out on his back, his hands behind his head, he watched *Sundance*'s masts describe an arc against the starry sky as her hull rocked in the slight swell. There was a luxurious double berth in the cabin below, but after a year of imprisonment he didn't know if he'd ever be able to sleep in a confined space again.

The cramped cell, the constant noise, and the lack of decent food or exercise had been no surprise, he thought. But the psychological impact had shocked and shaken him. He'd considered himself to be mentally tough and resilient, and to find those strengths called into question had been frightening. Doubt had eroded his self-belief, making him question his worthiness. Losing the love of his family, friends and, most devastatingly of all, his daughter had seemed like confirmation that he no longer mattered in a world that had moved on without him. The frustration of being wrongly accused, and of not being believed, had been almost unbearable.

As he'd grown used to the prison routine, his confusion and disbelief had crystallised into anger. He'd kept a grip on his sanity through the long days and nights by planning the voyage he would take when he won his freedom; by imagining how it would feel, guiding *Sundance* through the narrow inlet, into these calm waters again.

In the solitude of this safe anchorage was where he wanted to be. *Sundance* had taken a battering and it would take weeks to repair some of the damage and make her properly safe again. He'd treated her gently over the past few days, aware that another gale might be more than she could withstand.

The prospect of being forced to spend a month or more in this magical place was soothing. Here, he could confront the recent past with a level head and clear mind. While he worked to repair his beloved yacht, he could work on his own recovery, too. He needed a plan to put his shattered life back together in some sort of shape that would fit his changed future.

Beth Ashton put the copper coffee pot on the hob and ignited the flame beneath it. Then she padded in her bare feet across the tiled floor and slid the glass doors open, breathing in the scent of the herbs she'd planted in pots on the terrace and the ones that grew wild beyond it.

Two cups of Turkish coffee per day were her self-imposed limit, but the one she relished was the first one in the morning, sipped on the stone terrace as the sun rose over the headland to the east, reliably ushering in another perfect day. Wrapping her hands around the mug, she stepped out into the warm morning, and stopped.

Something was different. She placed the mug on the table and listened. Scanning the tree-covered slope that dropped away towards the beach, she tried to identify what had changed. Then it came again: the unmistakeable metallic tapping of metal rigging against a mast. Coffee forgotten, she peered through the scrubby trees and dense bushes, but one of the beauties of this place was the way the beach remained hidden from view until the last moment, when the stony path ended and the azure water and pristine shore burst into sight, dazzling in their perfection. She couldn't see anything.

During the weeks she'd spent at the villa, she hadn't seen a single vessel in the cove. The entrance, almost hidden, was narrow, requiring a level of navigational skill beyond most holiday-makers who might have hired a boat for the day. There were other bigger, easy-to-reach beaches up the coast.

Curious, and a little irritated at the interruption to the habitual rhythm of her day, Beth pulled the sarong she'd left by the pool around her, knotting it at the front. She slid her feet into her flip-flops and began to pick her way down the path towards the beach.

The tap-tap sound of the rigging grew louder but there were no accompanying voices, or the splash of swimmers. She slowed, and stopped in the shade of the pine trees that fringed the beach.

The yacht was elegant. Its sleek white hull, punctuated with portholes, swung gently on an anchor chain. She thought the design, with the foremast taller than the aft, meant it was called a ketch. The sails were tightly furled and there was no sign of life on the deck. Had the occupants already swum ashore and scrambled up the path, past her villa while she slept? A knot of unease tightened in her abdomen at the thought. She stepped out from under the trees and raised a hand to shade her eyes, wishing she'd thought to pick up her sunglasses.

A movement made her draw back sharply. A man, tall and wide-shouldered, had risen from the deck and now stood looking, or so it seemed, straight at her. She held her breath, hoping he hadn't seen her, not wanting to be noticed.

The only interactions she'd had since arriving five weeks previously had been with Omer in the village shop, relying heavily on the use of her phrase book, and the young girl who brought her lemon tea at the outside tables of the little café. The thought of a conversation with a stranger troubled and unnerved her. She squinted to see if she could recognise the flag at the stern of the boat, but it hung, limp and unmoving, in the early light, hiding its identity and, presumably, that of the owner of the vessel.

He, if he was the owner, remained motionless for a little longer. Then he moved to the stern. He extended his arms above his head and dived, in a graceful arc, cleaving the water with hardly a splash, and disappeared.

Something about the powerful lines of his silhouette and the clean execution of the dive kept Beth riveted to her spot. She scanned the glassy surface of the water but when he emerged it was in a completely different place from where she'd anticipated. The sound of his deep intake of breath carried to her across the water and she saw a shower of droplets sparkle in the low rays of the sun as he shook his head and then swam slowly back towards the ladder that extended down the side of his boat.

Was he alone, she wondered, as she watched him haul himself up the ladder onto the deck and lean against the foremast, looking towards the shore again. Surely a boat like that required more than one person to sail it. Perhaps his companion, because he must have one, was still asleep.

Perhaps there was more than one. She imagined a noisy, young crowd plunging into the water, swimming ashore and playing raucous games of volleyball or cricket on what she thought of as *her* beach.

Or perhaps, she thought, trying to put a positive spin on this intrusion, they'd move on when they realised there was nothing here for them. No ice cream or kebab sellers, or even a supply of fresh water. She shrank back into the deeper shadow of the trees and turned towards the path. She'd stay at home this morning; skip her usual morning swim in the sea and take it in the pool instead. By this afternoon, when she ventured back to the beach, she hoped she'd find solitude restored to the cove, with all trace of the unwelcome yacht and its crew erased.

Her coffee was cold. She threw it out onto the grass and began the process of making a fresh cup. She sipped at it, seated on the terrace, inhaling its intense, rich aroma, but the serenity she'd fought to cultivate over the past weeks eluded her. She'd arrived at the villa with her nerves in shreds, her life upended in a way she'd never anticipated, and her self-confidence pulverised.

The basic supplies she'd picked up at the airport had lasted a couple of days and it was hunger for something other than cheese crackers that had forced her to visit the village. There was a bicycle in the storeroom, the comprehensive villa

notes told her, for cycling along the rough track to
Sula. How long was it since she'd ridden a bicycle? Decades. She'd doubted she'd be able to balance for more than a few seconds. Balance was
an important ability to maintain as one aged, and
she practised it assiduously in her weekly yoga
class and when pulling on her tights or socks in
the mornings. But the idea of balancing on a bicycle had felt daunting. If she fell off onto the stony
track and broke something, who would find her?

For the first time, she'd questioned the wis-
dom of accepting Janet's offer of the empty villa,
'for as long as you need it, Beth'. Had Janet simply been trying to move her on from the guest
room she'd occupied for three weeks while her
life imploded? She knew that wasn't true, but
since everything had begun to go wrong, she'd
had difficulty in seeing the positive side to anything. If there was a positive side to being unexpectedly homeless and shockingly unemployed,
she personally had failed to find it.

The house in Islington, where she'd lived, first
with her parents, although she could barely remember her mother, and then with her father and
stepmother, was no longer home. It seemed her
father's dying promise that it would eventually
be hers carried no weight with her stepmother.
She'd bequeathed it to her only daughter, Beth's
half-sister, who now intended to sell it.

It shouldn't have mattered. It would have freed

Beth up to move in with her lover; to take their relationship to the next level; to commit to each other fully. Only that hadn't suited him at all, because it turned out he was fully committed already, to a wife in New York, on the Upper East Side.

The company where she'd steadily climbed the career ladder for twenty-five years, until she was appointed PA to a senior partner, had no longer felt like a safe place. How had she been so easily taken in? She'd resigned, with immediate effect, but as the heavy glass doors had swung closed behind her, she'd been engulfed in panic. Her home would soon no longer exist, and she'd left the job that had given her identity for so long. She'd felt invisible.

Fumbling for her phone with numb fingers, she'd called her best friend, Janet.

Several days after arriving at the villa, the thought of biting into a crisp slice of one of the watermelons she'd seen, stacked like footballs at roadside stalls, in the taxi ride from the airport, got the better of her. She'd wheeled out the bicycle and launched herself on a few trial runs across the dry grass behind the house. The bike had wobbled alarmingly, but she hadn't landed face down in the dust, and so she'd loaded a shopping bag into the basket on the handlebars and set off down the track in search of food.

The enjoyment of her solitude had grown with

each day and now the idea of having to engage with the visitor to the cove filled her with unease. How, she wondered, had she come to this? Had the crushing of her expectations and the loss of her job crushed her personality, too? Reluctantly, she admitted the truth. The energetic carer she'd been to her aged stepmother, and the capable PA in a challenging role, had turned into an indecisive, anxious shadow. She was supposed to be using this time to rebuild her life, but so far all she had done was withdraw further and further into herself, with no idea of how she was going to move forward. What would happen when she had to leave and return to London? She pushed the thought away and drained the coffee mug. Janet had said she could stay here for as long as she needed, and it was only early July.

But she made a decision to log on to the Internet later and start searching for a new job. Even though she had no plans to leave soon, she had to confront the reality of her future. And the more immediate reality of confronting the broad-shouldered man on the boat was too unnerving to contemplate just yet.

CHAPTER TWO

THE INTENSE HEAT of the afternoon had begun to fade, and the light had softened when Beth ventured down to the beach again. The thought of being seen in her cherry-red bikini had almost made her change into her black one-piece swimsuit, so, just in case she met anyone, she'd pulled a thigh-length cotton kaftan over it. If the boat had gone, as she really hoped it had, she'd be able to have a swim in private and not care about exposing her body to the eyes of strangers.

Janet had bought the bikini for her, placing it, still wrapped in tissue, on top of her clothes in the suitcase.

'I saw it and thought of you, Beth,' she'd said, moving a pile of underwear from the chair so she could perch on the edge of it. 'It's your colour, and you deserve a treat.'

'Do I?' Beth had lifted the silky bandeau top from its wrapping and shaken her head. 'I've never worn a bikini, Janet, and I can't start now.' She'd glanced down at her body. 'I'd be so self-conscious.'

'Why?' Janet had sounded surprised. 'You've got a gorgeous figure.'

Beth had run a hand over the curve of her hips. 'I'd gained a little weight recently, although I've probably lost it now…'

'You were too thin before. You're perfect just as you are now. And anyway, you'll have the pool and probably the beach all to yourself. There'll be no one else to see you, so be daring. Wear the bikini!' Janet had given her a quick hug. 'You have nothing to be self-conscious about at all.'

As she picked her way down the rough path a dislodged pebble rattled ahead of her, and she paused, tugging at the hem of the kaftan. Should she return to the villa and dig out the old one-piece, after all? But Janet's words echoed in her head, and she lifted her chin, took a breath and carried on.

The ketch had not gone.

It floated, on its own perfect, upside-down reflection, in the middle of the cove, and it appeared to be deserted. The air was so still that even the tap of the rigging had been silenced. Earlier, as she'd dozed on the shady terrace, Beth had heard the putter of an outboard motor, but it had sounded distant, through the heavy afternoon air. Now she wondered if the crew of the mysterious boat had taken to a dinghy and motored up the coast, in search of a livelier neighbourhood.

She stepped out of the shade of the trees and

onto the beach. Her eyes had been fixed on the boat so she didn't notice the man floating on his back in the water until it was too late. He stood, water streaming from his broad, bronzed body, and began to wade out of the sea towards her. She froze, fixed to the spot, wanting to turn away but determined to stand her ground.

'Good afternoon.' The voice was deep and slightly roughened, as if rusty from lack of use. Apprehension sent goosebumps racing over her skin. She was sharply aware of how isolated and vulnerable she was. She shifted her balance on the pebbles beneath her flip-flops. She'd have to kick them off if she had to run...

He was silhouetted against the low evening sun, but she recognised him immediately as the man she'd seen dive into the sea earlier. His broad shoulders were square, his stance upright and, when he stopped a little way in front of her, he folded muscled arms across his chest.

'I hope I didn't startle you.'

She raised her eyes, squinting into the sun, even though she was wearing her sunglasses. Her heartbeat, which had leapt into overdrive in response to a shot of adrenaline, steadied to something more like normal and she tried to quieten her breathing.

Beth swallowed. 'I... Good afternoon. I haven't met any strangers here before. I'm just...surprised.'

'I apologise.'

Putting on the kaftan had been the right decision.

He stood at least six inches taller than her own five feet eight, and his clipped, cultured English was at odds with his slightly piratical appearance. His dark hair, threaded with silver, looked as if it hadn't been cut for many weeks and he raised one hand and shoved his fingers through it, slicking seawater down his back. Thick dark stubble, lightened with grey, roughened his jaw. If there were lines at the outer corners of his eyes, they were hidden behind his Ray-Bans. Big hands rested on the muscles of his upper arms.

She dropped her eyes, aware that she was staring. He had the sort of suntan that resulted from weeks of exposure to the weather, not a few days at a beach resort. Dripping-wet board shorts covered his thighs. A livid gash ran from his left knee down his shin and although the cut had healed over, the bruising surrounding the injury looked angry.

'What happened to your leg?' If she'd intended to say anything, that wasn't it, but the sight of the laceration had shocked her into speech.

He glanced down, shaking his head. 'I tripped over a line on the deck and caught it on a cleat.'

'It looks nasty.'

'It was a nasty moment. Price you pay for sailing a forty-footer solo in a force eight.'

Beth's eyes shifted beyond him, to the ketch. Her white hull was tinged with the pale gold of the sinking sun. She looked elegant and serene.

'Solo? You don't have a crew?'

'No. Not this time.' He turned away from her, following her gaze. 'It makes the sailing harder, but the solitude is the pay-off.' His voice had dropped.

A little flash of hope warmed Beth's insides. When he discovered this was her cove, he'd move on to somewhere he didn't have to share.

'You won't be staying long, then,' she said to his back. 'There's nothing here.'

He glanced at her over his shoulder, one eyebrow raised. 'I know that.' He shrugged. 'That's the appeal. I took the RIB down the coast this afternoon. The shop in the village stocks everything I need.'

'Oh. Do you know the area?'

'This coast? Like the back of my hand. But it's been a few years since my last visit.'

Beth thought she heard the grate of anger in his tone, and she moved away a little, wary, and anxious to put him off.

'Things change,' she said. 'If it's solitude you're after, you'll have to find somewhere else, because I come to this beach every day, and I like my privacy, too.'

She felt the satisfaction of seeing his mouth

tighten. If she'd been able to see his eyes she felt sure they would have registered surprise.

'Every day?' he said. 'How do you get here? You don't have a boat and it's a tough walk along the track to the village.'

'As I said, things change. There's a villa up there now.' She indicated the tree-covered slope behind them. 'It belongs to a friend of mine and I'm there for…for the summer,' she said, firmly.

'So it was you, this morning.'

'I didn't think you'd seen me.'

'You moved, and then your shadow didn't fit with your surroundings.'

In the silence that followed, Beth was aware of the quiet slap of the sea on the pebbles and the sigh of a breeze through the pines. He held himself very still. She wished he'd remove his shades so she could read his expression more easily but remembered that she still wore her own.

'A villa?' He sounded incredulous, and not a bit pleased. 'Is it big? How many of you are there?'

'Big enough, but it's just me.' Mentally, Beth kicked herself for telling him she was on her own, but it was too late. 'It's only been finished a couple of months. My friend's husband, Emin, is half Turkish and they intended to spend the summer here with their family. But work commitments have kept them in London.'

She saw some of the tension leave his shoulders.

'What,' he asked, 'made you opt to spend several months alone at the end of an almost impassable track?' He shook his head. 'At the height of summer.'

'Possibly,' she said, 'something similar to what made you decide to undertake an obviously hazardous voyage—' she looked down at his injured leg '—solo, in search of solitude.'

'Touché.' A line between his dark brows deepened. 'It seems we're both annoyed at having our space invaded. Perhaps we can reach an agreement.'

'Perhaps you can find another isolated cove. Your home is mobile. I can't move anywhere else.'

He unfolded his arms and pushed his hands into the pockets of his shorts. 'No.' He shook his head, once. 'I can't move, either.' He looked across the water at the boat. 'I pushed her, too hard, to get here. There're repairs which need to be done before she'll be safe to sail anywhere else.' He glanced down at his injured leg. 'And I'm tired.' He rotated his left shoulder. 'And hurt. I need to recover. And this is the place I want to be. I need...'

Beth felt a bubble of frustration expand in her chest. He was unreasonable. 'Surely there must be somewhere...' she began, but he raised a hand and stopped her.

'We've established one thing. Neither of us is going anywhere. What we need to do is work out how to avoid each other. When do you prefer to use the beach?'

Beth wanted to use the beach when she felt like it. She had fallen into the habit of swimming in the cove after her first coffee and before breakfast, before the heat climbed to a level that made being on the beach uncomfortable. Then, in the late afternoon, she'd stroll down again and swim while watching the sun sink in the west and the sea and sky turn from blue to aquamarine to indigo. When Venus appeared, always the first gleaming jewel to adorn the evening sky, she'd climb the path back up to the villa for the evening. She nibbled at her bottom lip, trying to suppress her annoyance.

'Usually in the mornings...'

'I presume you don't spend all day on the beach.' She felt his scrutiny travel over her and thought about the sprinkling of freckles that dusted her nose, in spite of her addiction to sunscreen. 'You obviously protect yourself from the sun.'

'Too much exposure to the sun is dangerous.' She lifted her chin. Even at this time of the afternoon, she could feel her legs burning. 'Perhaps you should consider that.' She cringed at the primness she heard in her own voice.

Unexpectedly, he smiled. Even white teeth gleamed in his bronzed face.

'Perhaps I should.' He pulled a hand along his

jaw, the stubble rasping under his palm. 'I'll string an awning up over the deck for some shade.'

Beth felt colour rising into her cheeks at the faint note of teasing in his tone. She raised a hand and lifted her heavy hair off her neck, wishing she'd tied it up.

'I come to the beach early in the morning and in the late afternoon, to avoid the most intense heat of the day.'

'That's easy, then,' he said. 'I'll avoid the beach at those times. We need never speak to each other.'

'But...you'll be watching me, from the deck, waiting for me to leave...'

'That's a problem?'

If only you knew, thought Beth furiously.

She wouldn't be able to wear the red bikini anymore. Not if she thought someone—*he*—was watching her. Anxiety, which she'd managed to bury under the calm, measured routine she'd imposed on herself, stirred, reminding her it might have retreated but it had not gone away.

'I wouldn't be able to relax,' she muttered, turning away from him and starting to walk towards the beginning of the path.

'Hey.' His voice behind her was softer and a little warmer. She hesitated and turned back. 'I... I'm sorry. I've invaded your space and your privacy.' He raised a hand and pulled his shades from his face, pinching the bridge of his nose between his thumb and finger. 'And yes, I understand you'd feel uncomfortable if you thought I was watching you, so I promise that I won't. It's just that I'm stuck here, the same as you are, until she's ready to sail again.'

His eyes were dark, she now saw, dark blue, and troubled. His hands were back in his pockets, his knees and shoulders braced as if he was holding fatigue at bay by sheer willpower.

An unexpected wave of sympathy for him washed over her. She appreciated his apology and identified with his position. Something had driven him to reach this place and it hadn't turned out as he'd expected and now the impetus had faded. He looked sad and drained of energy.

'Thanks.' She nodded. 'I appreciate that.' It occurred to her that he might need help, but she dismissed the thought. How could she be useful to a man like him, who sailed single-handed and relied on his own resourcefulness for survival? And anyway, he'd said he wanted solitude. She turned away, but his voice came from behind her.

'I don't know your name.'

'Since we're never going to speak to each other again you don't need to,' she threw over her shoulder.

CHAPTER THREE

IT WAS THREE days since Jensen had watched her walk away into the trees and disappear up the slope. The set of her shoulders had been stiff and she'd held her head high. It looked as if she was making an effort to appear offhand.

He hadn't seen her again.

The plan worked, he thought.

Solitude was what he wanted; what he craved. He didn't plan to expend any energy on thinking about a woman who wished he were somewhere else. Why, then, did he feel a little uneasy?

He hadn't exactly looked for her, in the mornings and evenings, when she could have been on the beach or swimming in the crystalline waters of the cove. But he'd noticed that she wasn't there.

He hadn't meant to frighten her off, if that was what had happened. The little twinge of guilt he felt surprised him. This was why, he thought, the days of tough sailing had been so good. So *welcome.* On those days he'd been in sole control of *Sundance,* and his own destiny. There'd been no time or space for feelings and emotions. He'd learned to keep them fiercely battened down while he'd been imprisoned but now found he had little control over them, when they chose to ambush him when he least expected it.

It was the morning of day three. Jensen leaned on the rail of *Sundance* and scanned the curved shoreline, narrowing his eyes as he searched the fringe of trees that bordered it. The heat was already building, promising a scorching day. Perhaps she had come down for a swim before the sun had risen.

He dismissed that idea as impossible. Even if she'd tried her best to avoid his attention, the splash of her wading into the water would have alerted him. He was acutely attuned to the rhythm of the movement of the sea, and he would have noticed a change in it at once.

He was certain she hadn't been onto the beach since their exchange of words, and that niggle of guilt stirred his conscience, again. He'd probably made her feel insecure...maybe even unsafe. He'd appeared out of nowhere, as far as she was concerned, invading her privacy. She was alone, in an isolated place, and the last time he'd glanced at his reflection in a mirror, he'd looked far from friendly or even civilised. The realisation that he'd most likely frightened her bothered him.

To his disappointment, he hadn't been able to relax as completely as he'd expected. He'd been on the move for a month, he told himself, with reaching this place his one goal. It'd take time to adjust to staying still. *'I wouldn't be able to relax,'* she'd said, and now he couldn't, either. He suspected it was because he knew someone else—the woman in the thin cotton kaftan, which did a bad job of hiding her curves and the red bikini she wore beneath it—was somewhere up there, behind the trees.

If he knew her name, would he be able to put their encounter behind him, neatly tidied away where he didn't have to think about it again?

He straightened up, dragging his fingers through his hair and shutting down those thoughts. Her name and her curves were irrelevant, even if, in the past—the quite recent past—the latter would have sent a dart of anticipation and appreciation through him. He was beyond any of that. Those days were behind him.

He'd rather she wasn't there, and he knew she felt the same about him. If she'd chosen not to visit the beach, it was her decision. From the deck of *Sundance* nothing about the secret cove had changed and the solitude he craved was intact.

He'd go for his morning swim and then put the awning up over the foredeck, as he'd said he would. When he'd finished, the shade would be welcome as the temperature climbed towards forty degrees and he'd get on with the list of repairs he needed to make to *Sundance*.

* * *

When she realised that she'd read the same paragraph three times, Beth closed her book and dropped it onto the paved terrace beside her sun lounger.

Even a thriller set in the snowy wastes of Alaska couldn't distract her from the heat. She swallowed a mouthful of water from the glass at her elbow. The ice had melted, and the drink was tepid.

She stood and walked over to the pool, stepped carefully onto the Roman steps and sat down. The water was too warm to be refreshing and she longed for another swim in the sea. However hot the day grew, the sea temperature remained just cool enough, but she no longer wanted to venture onto the beach.

Each morning, she heard the telltale chink of the rigging tapping against the mast, reminding her that the boat was there.

She sighed and stretched her legs out in front of her, wriggling her toes. The opalescent polish on her toenails looked pretty against her pale gold skin. Despite keeping to the shade when at all possible, she'd acquired a light tan, even on her feet. Bracing her arms, she leaned back and studied the rest of her body.

Her thighs and tummy looked toned, which must be a result of all the swimming she was doing and the cycling trips to the village. The heat had been intense earlier and she'd taken a cool shower and had a siesta when she'd returned with fresh fruit and vegetables in the basket of the bicycle. Those last few weeks in London had been confusing and chaotic and her exercise routine had been forgotten, but she felt better now that she'd established it again.

From the time her father, his health failing, had charged her with the care of her stepmother and half-sister she'd begun to accept she'd never have the freedom to meet a partner, fall in love, or have children. The fairy tale didn't happen for everyone. Her role had been to work to provide for them, and she had fulfilled it. Her father had left them the house to live in with the promise that it would be hers, one day, but not much else.

There had been no reason why her future shouldn't have been exactly as she'd expected it to be, until she'd been foolish enough to believe she could be special to someone.

She wriggled forwards and sank into the water. She'd swim some laps to work up an appetite for her evening meal and then eat it out on the terrace. With luck, a light breeze might pick up to take the edge off the heat.

The stranger from the boat had not disturbed her, at least not physically. She'd thought curiosity might have driven him to climb up through the trees to see the villa, but he'd respected her desire for privacy, as she had his. His look of exhaustion, though, and the memory of his injured leg, plagued her thoughts. He'd turned down her tentative offer of help, but she'd like to know he was all right. Then she thought she'd be able to put him out of her mind.

Swimming was supremely calming. The measured strokes of her arms, the kick of her legs and the steady breathing all combined to create an even rhythm and, once she hit her stride, she could continue indefinitely.

Twilight had descended by the time she took a deep breath, dived beneath the surface and swam the final length of the pool underwater. As she emerged, in a rush of exhaled air and with water streaming down her face and throat, she heard someone call.

Sinking back into the water, Beth pushed her hair back from her face and peered across the shadowed garden, apprehension snaking up her spine. But the shape of the man who stood on the grass, between the pool and the trees, was instantly recognisable. It felt as though she'd conjured him up with the power of thought.

'Hi.' Her greeting was guarded. She stayed in the water as he walked towards the pool.

'I'm sorry to disturb you. I know you don't want company. I just…'

Beth shook her head. 'That's…okay.' She remained where she was, with only her head and shoulders above the water, as he stopped at the edge.

She allowed her eyes to travel from his bronzed,

bare feet up his legs. His injured shin looked inflamed, she thought. Faded shorts rested low on his hips. His hands were shoved into the pockets, but he pulled one out and ran it through his untidy hair, the movement drawing Beth's attention to the flex of his biceps, and the bunching of the muscles of his chest. His body looked hard, his abdomen tight and toned. The light smattering of dark hair, mixed with grey, did not hide the gleam of his tanned, smooth skin.

She felt an unfamiliar, and unwelcome, stirring somewhere deep in her body, and a sudden constriction of her lungs stopped her from taking a breath deep enough to quell the little tingle of awareness that shivered through her.

'I'm sorry,' he said, again. 'I just wondered if you're all right. You haven't been to the beach.'

'No. I—' Beth realised she was staring. She made an effort to drag her eyes away, but it felt as if there was nowhere to look, apart from at him.

'But I can see that you're fine. I'll leave.'

'I just haven't felt comfortable about the beach. I'd be intruding on your space.'

'We made a plan.'

She shrugged. 'Actually, you made the plan. I decided it didn't really suit me.'

'I promised not to watch you.'

'You did. But…'

'But you didn't trust me to keep my word.' He nodded. 'I get that. Why would you?'

'Oh. It's not that. I know you came here looking for seclusion, just as I did, so I didn't want to
disturb you. You haven't disturbed me, either.'

'Until now.'

His eyes met hers and then he raised his head
and stepped back.

'You're not disturbing me. I've finished my
swim.' She felt suddenly self-conscious, remembering that she was wearing the revealing bikini
and that within a few minutes the underwater
lighting of the pool would come on automatically.
She'd be lit up like a fish in a tank. A fish with
too many curves, wearing a too-small, look-at-me,
bright red bikini. She'd have to get out before that
happened. 'But as for being alright, your leg looks
as if it should be seen by a doctor.'

He glanced down at the injury. 'Yeah. You're
probably right. It doesn't feel too good. Do you
know if there's a clinic in Sula?'

'The information pack in the villa will probably include details of local medical facilities. I
can have a look if you like.'

She began to move towards the steps, eyeing
the distance to her sarong, which she'd dropped
next to her book on the terrace. If she could reach
it and wrap herself up, she'd feel a whole lot better.

'That's very kind. Thank you.'

Beth felt for the steps and put her feet on the
lowest one. As she straightened her legs the upper

part of her body left the water. Acutely aware of the smallness of the bikini and how it was more revealing wet than dry, she sank down again.

His eyes rested on her for a moment and then he turned, covering the distance to the sunbed in three strides. In a matter of seconds, he'd gathered up her sarong and skirted the pool. He stood at the top of the steps, holding the length of fabric stretched out between his hands.

'Here you are,' he said quietly. 'You can get out now. But if you'd rather I went away, I'll go.'

'It's…okay.' In spite of the warmth of the water and the evening air, she shivered.

'Are you cold?'

'No. Not cold. It's just…you surprised me a little. I wasn't expecting a visitor.'

'I didn't want to frighten you. I heard you swimming, and so I called out.' He shook the sarong gently. 'Would you like to come out? Or if you'd rather I left, I'll go.'

Beth climbed up the steps, hunching her shoulders and focussing on her feet. As she reached the edge of the pool, her eyes still fixed on the ground, she felt the feather-light sarong settle over her shoulders. She grabbed the edges and pulled it around herself, bunching the fabric in her fists under her chin.

'Thank you.' Her voice felt tight and strained.

The pool water was running down her back, puddling at her feet. She wanted to squeeze her hair and wring it out but she didn't dare loosen her grip on the fabric that was shielding her.

'Do you want to go and get dressed?' He'd turned away from her and was studying the villa.

Beth nodded. 'I'll be back in a minute.' She transferred the sarong to her left hand and wiped the water from her eyes, pushing her hair off her forehead.

In the fading light his profile was becoming blurred, but she could make out his strong, slightly Roman nose and straight, dark brows. She wondered what his mouth looked like, beneath the scruff. And were his eyes really that dark or was it simply the lack of light that intensified their colour?

As if on cue, the pool lights came on, casting a watery glow over the immediate surroundings.

'Half past six,' she said, gesturing towards the pool. 'That's the time the lights come on.'

He nodded. 'And what do you usually do at six-thirty? Have a drink? Cook a meal?' She wondered if he was teasing her. 'You seem to keep to a set timetable, even here in the wilds of Turkey.'

'It's how I live. How I've always lived. Making the best use of my time.'

A little flare of anxiety ignited in her chest. She'd managed to curb it by establishing her routine here and this man had already upset it once. Over the past three days she'd made adjustments, allowances. The changes weren't perfect, but she could manage while he remained.

Keeping to her routines meant she had her life under control, superficially, at least.

He lifted his shoulders and dropped them again, his hands back in his pockets. 'Time is irrelevant here. Accepting that fact is liberating. And a great luxury.'

To her surprise, Beth felt the burn of anxiety fade a little. She'd regarded this intrusion as a threat, not only to herself personally, but to the way she'd chosen to live here. But he wasn't dangerous. He'd come, he said, to see if she was all right.

It felt like a long time since anyone had asked her that.

Janet had taken her into her home and supported her while her life had unravelled around her. *'You'll get through this, Beth. You'll be all right,'* had become her refrain during those fraught weeks.

Everyone had always assumed she'd be all right. She was dependable. Strong and organised. The thought that she might not be okay was unthinkable. But what if she wasn't?

Facing her vulnerability and accepting it had been hard, but she knew it was the first step towards moving on with her life.

Suddenly, she didn't want this man to walk away into the gathering darkness. The chance to have a conversation with someone felt like one she would like to take.

She glanced down at the puddle that had formed around her feet. 'Will you wait?' She nodded towards the table and chairs on the terrace. 'I'll be right back.'

Jensen chose not to sit down. Instead, he walked to the edge of the terrace and looked out over the tops of the trees. The two headlands that sheltered the cove were visible as darker masses against the paler sky. The air was heavy and still, with no hint of a breeze.

He exhaled, trying to relax his tense muscles, then breathed in, relishing the aroma of the herbs that grew nearby, as they released their scents onto the warm air after the heat of the day.

He heard her light footstep on the terrace and turned. She'd changed into a loose cotton, long-sleeved midi dress in a shade of dark green. It floated around her as she walked, masterfully disguising her shape. The most vivid imagination wouldn't have conjured up the gentle curves he knew were hidden beneath it.

Irritation at his thoughts made him slap them away. He felt under-dressed and wished he had a tee shirt on, at least. Sucking in a breath, he strolled towards her.

'Shall we start again?' He held out his hand. 'Jensen.'

Her hesitation was slight but noticeable. Then she put her hand in his, briefly, before withdrawing it abruptly.

'Beth.'

For the first time, in the soft lighting of the terrace, he saw that her eyes were green, fringed with dark lashes and faint smile lines at the corners. She must have rubbed her hair dry because it was no longer dripping, and she'd twisted it up into a loose knot.

'Pleased to meet you, Beth.'

'Oh, I don't think you are, Jensen.' The slight lift of the corners of her mouth softened her words. 'You wish I weren't here. Or the house, either.'

'That is true. Just as you wish *Sundance* and I would sail away into the sunset, leaving you with your own private beach.'

'*Sundance*? Is that the name of your yacht?' She placed a small brown glass pot on the table.

'It is.' He nodded. 'And the sun set a while ago, so that option has gone for another day.'

She shrugged. 'Maybe tomorrow…?'

'Maybe not.' He shook his head. 'And you?'

'The furthest I'm going in the near future will be Sula.' She put her hands on the back of one of the wooden chairs. Her fingers were long and slim. No rings, he noticed. 'Would you like to sit down? For a few minutes?'

Jensen hesitated. 'I wouldn't want to interrupt your plans for the evening.'

A dimple indented her left cheek, but it faded as quickly as it had appeared.

'I think I can spare the time. My plans can be flexible. A little.'

She pulled out a chair and he followed, seating himself opposite her, across the table.

'How,' he asked, with genuine interest, 'do you get to the village? I remember the track and it's a tough walk, especially in the summer. Some bits of it are steep and there's no shade, to speak of.'

'There's a bicycle that comes with the villa. It's not an easy ride but I've grown used to it now and I rather enjoy the challenge. I go early, to avoid the worst of the heat. It's helping to keep me fit.'

'You need help with that?'

'Here I do, yes. In London…' She stopped, leaning back in the chair and putting a hand up to her hair, as if to check it was still in place.

'You live in London? I suppose you belong to a fancy gym where you run on a treadmill and lift weights.' He looked around, thinking of the state-of-the-art gym and swimming pool in the basement of his former office building. 'A far cry from here.'

'Yes.' She nodded. 'That is, yes, I live in London. Or I did. But I've never belonged to a gym.' She reached out and nudged the glass jar towards him. 'Rub this on your shin. It's comfrey cream. Excellent for bruising.'

He picked it up and studied the printed label.

'Thank you. I'll try it.' His eyes found hers. 'Do you know of other herbal remedies?'

'Plant uses interest me, both in cooking and for medicinal purposes. I'm going to do…was planning to do a course in herbology.'

Some change had impacted on her life, he thought, but he pretended not to notice her slip. It would be wrong to probe and anyway he didn't need to know the details. He'd just wanted to know she was all right.

'I should probably go.'

Beth nodded. He felt better knowing her name. She seemed to feel a lot more relaxed since she'd returned, wearing that dress.

'I had a look at the file. Apparently Omer at the shop will be able to tell you where to go for medical help. He's the cousin of the owner of the villa and he seems to know everything and everyone. Will you go tomorrow?'

Jensen nodded. 'I will. I'll take the RIB.'

'I've heard an outboard motor a couple of times.'

'Has it disturbed you?'

'Not at all. Before I knew you were a lone sailor, I pictured a rowdy crowd of twenty-somethings roaring off to find the latest beach party.' She shrugged. '*That* would have been disturbing.'

'I brought the RIB up onto the beach. If I'd thought I was going to be sitting down at a table in such a civilised way I would at least have put on a tee shirt.'

He liked the sound of her quiet laugh. It was gentle and musical and he thought he'd like to hear it again. She tipped her head back, exposing the smooth column of her neck.

'I haven't entertained anyone here before. I haven't even *spoken* to anyone, apart from Omer in the shop and Ela at the café. That's why I like to cycle over there quite regularly. Otherwise, I might forget what civilised looks like.'

'Let me tell you, then, that, from the point of view of someone who has been sailing single-handed for over a month, civilised looks very much like this.' The gesture of his outstretched arm encompassed the terrace, the pool and the smiling woman across the table.

'Thank you.' She looked down at her hands, clasped loosely together on the table in front of her. 'Would you…?'

'I should go…'

'I was going to ask if you'd like a slice of watermelon. I bought one this morning and it's perfectly ripe.' Her words seemed to come out in a rush, as if she'd been uncertain about saying them and had then let them out before she could change her mind.

He'd been about to stand up, but he relaxed back into the chair. He nodded. 'If you're sure, I'd love some.' Then he wondered if he should have refused her offer. The longer he stayed, the more comfortable he'd feel, and he didn't want comfortable companionship. He wanted to be alone.

But Beth had already disappeared in the direction of the kitchen. She returned with plates, paper napkins and slices of pink watermelon in a bowl.

'Help yourself. It's delicious.'

It was. It was crisp, sweet and so juicy that their hands were soon sticky. Jensen couldn't remember anything ever tasting quite so good.

'Thank you, Beth.' He pushed his chair back and stood. 'I didn't intend to take up so much of your time.'

'Thank you for checking up on me.' She stood and stretched out her hand. He took it, feeling her slender fingers, sticky with watermelon juice, against his rough palm. She pulled her hand away and laughed again. 'It's impossible to eat watermelon and not get sticky.'

'Thank you for this.' He pocketed the pot of comfrey. He swung around and headed off into the darkness, finding his way to the place where the path tipped down the steep slope towards the cove. Before the shadow of the trees and scrub swallowed him up, he looked back. Beth stood where he'd left her, watching him leave. He raised an arm, hoping she'd be able to see him in the gloom, and when she gave a quick wave back he felt a small hit of satisfaction.

He needn't worry about her. She was fine.

* * *

Beth watched him—*Jensen*—leave. Meeting him again and learning his name had transformed him, in her mind, from the interloper to someone more approachable. She still wished he'd go away, or that he'd never come at all, but at least she knew he wasn't going to disrupt her quiet existence more than he had done already.

She watched as he dropped his arm and turned away into the darkness of the trees, then she went into the villa and pulled the sliding glass door closed, shutting out the dark and the hum of insect nightlife, which formed the background noise to every evening.

What had made her ask him to stay, even for a few minutes? To share the enjoyment of something as simple as a slice of watermelon? Although strength and self-reliance were the outward qualities that struck her first about him, it had been his underlying tentativeness that had made her look at him a little more carefully. There was an elusive quality of uncertainty about him, which she thought he probably wasn't even aware of himself, as if he needed her to recognise something in him and respond to it.

Was it as simple as him needing company after his solo voyage? If that was the case, why did he insist on being alone? And if he valued his privacy so much, why had he come to check up on her?

Nobody had ever needed her for herself and

she wondered how that felt. Was that what she glimpsed in Jensen? A need to be understood and accepted for himself, and himself alone, whoever that might be?

The open-plan living area of the villa had been designed to accommodate large groups. She imagined Janet planning get-togethers here, with family from England and Turkish cousins filling the house with laughter, the terrace echoing with the shrieks of young people enjoying the pool. It was the perfect place for reunions or celebrations.

Upstairs, the cool, calm bedrooms would accommodate couples and their children.

Beth shook herself mentally and pulled open the door of the large fridge, extracting a bottle of wine from the rack. She half filled one of the heavy, stemmed glasses and stretched out on a sofa from where she could see the terrace and the pool, and the trees beyond.

She thought about what she might have for dinner. Taking a sip of the cold, crisp wine, she relished the feeling of it in her mouth and throat. She'd briefly thought of inviting him to stay for a meal, but was glad she hadn't. Neither of them wanted company and it would have felt awkward. She'd given him the comfrey cream and they'd enjoyed a few minutes together. That was enough.

She pictured him steering the RIB across the

dark water towards *Sundance*, climbing aboard and then perhaps turning to look back at the trees, where he could now imagine her at the villa.

The images were disturbing, along with the faint regret that accompanied them. She reached up and released her hair from the untidy knot, irritably shaking it out around her shoulders.

Perhaps it was time to cut it short. Working long hours had meant it was convenient to be able to put it up in a severe, neat pleat rather than to have to style it every day.

She'd seen a Turkish barber in the village. Perhaps they'd cut it for her. She'd enquire tomorrow. She wondered if her phrasebook would stretch to 'bob'.

CHAPTER FOUR

THE GIRL AT the café, whose name she'd discovered was Ela, brought Beth a tray of tea without her having to order it. She'd come to anticipate the morning tea ritual, on the days when she visited the village, almost as much as she craved that first cup of Turkish coffee first thing in the mornings at the villa.

She loved the silver pots, containing the brewed tea and hot water, the delicate, slim-waisted tea glasses and the plates on which they rested. A spoon, for lifting up the tiny lemon wedges, lay at the side. Today, Ela placed a small bowl containing squares of baklava at her elbow, waving away Beth's protestations.

Beth flipped open her laptop and logged onto the café's Internet. There was Wi-Fi at the villa, but it was unreliable, and this morning had been non-existent. Besides, she'd found she enjoyed sitting in the shade outside the café with the buzz of village life in the background. She opened the file containing her CV.

It was orderly and utterly dull. The only bit of it that caused her spirits to lift, slightly, was where she'd listed her hobby as 'gardening'.

Apart from a few temporary jobs, after she'd left her secretarial college, she'd worked for the same company for twenty-five years.

It had been a safe, predictable job, at least to begin with. She could walk to the offices in the City from the house in Islington, passing a supermarket on the way home.

The document on the screen in front of her showed her steady progress up through the ranks of the administration staff, with regular promotions that had brought added responsibilities and benefits.

What changes could she make to it that would cause a possible new employer to take notice? And what positive spin could she put on the facts so that her abrupt departure would seem like a good thing?

She poured tea into the pleasing glass and topped it up with hot water. From her table under the shade cloth that stretched over the rickety veranda of the café, she watched the morning unfold in the village square. A heat haze already shimmered above the roofs of the market stalls.

Across the square, a knot of men gathered outside the barber shop, waiting for it to open. She was glad she'd pinned her hair up again this morning, leaving her neck and shoulders open to any breeze that might stir. But the idea of walking into the barber's and trying to explain that she wanted her hair cut off felt daunting. She'd draw attention to herself, be the subject of rapid-fire conversation between the other customers, some of whom would potentially express a loud opinion, which she would not be able to understand.

Perhaps she could wait until there was a quiet moment, between customers. Or break the habit of a month and come into the village later in the afternoon, after the siesta and before the locals took their evening strolls.

She must try not to overthink everything. The habit added layers of unnecessary worry to every day. How much easier life would be if she could be spontaneous, and not care about what other people thought.

The aroma of the hot, lemony tea permeated her senses as she took a sip, closing her eyes to concentrate on its full impact.

When she opened them, she saw Jensen cross the square and enter the shop, his broad frame pausing briefly in the doorway, before disappearing into the dark interior. She closed her laptop.

A minute later, he emerged, with Omer at his shoulder, pointing across the square and looking at his watch. Beth stood up as Jensen began to walk in her direction.

He hesitated when he saw her and for a second she thought he was going to greet her and then simply carry on walking, but he stopped, a smile lifting the corners of his mouth.

'How is your leg?' She glanced down at his shin, which looked shiny. 'You've used the comfrey?'

He nodded. 'I have. And Omer has given me directions to the clinic. It opens in an hour.'

'He seems to be the lynchpin on which everyone depends.'

'He does.' He took another step towards her.

'Would you like to join me?' She indicated the second chair at the small round table. 'I'm having tea but if you'd prefer coffee...'

Jensen signalled to Ela, who was wiping down a table nearby, and ordered Turkish coffee. 'Are you working?' He glanced at her laptop.

'No. More like looking for work. But...' she pushed the laptop a little to the side and lifted her tea glass '...I'm uninspired. Have some baklava.' She took a piece in her fingers and bit into its sweet nuttiness. 'Mmm...' Then, suddenly aware of Jensen's eyes on her mouth, she bent her head and dabbed at her lips with a paper napkin.

He helped himself to a square, chewing slowly, and she watched his throat move as he swallowed.

'Thank you.' He lifted his coffee cup, tiny and delicate in his broad hand, and took a mouthful. 'The pharmacy is round the corner from the barber and it doubles up as the clinic, two days a week. Today is one of the days.' His brows drew together, the line between them furrowing.

'Is it still painful?'

'A bit.' He replaced the cup on its saucer and folded his arms. 'Thank you again for last evening. I didn't realise you were planning to come to the village today.'

Beth swallowed a mouthful of tea, keeping her eyes on the table, which was, she thought, much smaller than the one at which they'd sat last night. Even though they were outside, it suddenly felt rather intimate. 'I wasn't. But the Internet connection at the villa wasn't working this morning and I needed to…'

'Job hunt?'

'Yes.'

He removed his shades and rested his forearms on the table, leaning in towards her a little. His dark eyes were serious. 'You don't seem enthusiastic about it.'

'I'm not.' She tapped her laptop. 'As you can see, I've given up, for the day.' Beth shifted on her chair. Her pink linen dress, usually so cool and airy, felt clammy. She ran a hand across the back of her neck and patted her hair, checking it was still secure.

Jensen's eyes followed the movement and then he looked past her, across the square. 'If you want to talk about it…?'

'Oh, no. Thank you.' Inwardly, she shrank from

the idea of Jensen reading the dull catalogue of her working life to date. She began to think inviting him to join her had been a mistake. He was too close. The small shifts of expression on his face were intriguing, the silver threads in his dark hair gleamed in the bright light, and, at this close range, his eyes were navy blue.

Awareness, unfamiliar and tantalising, seemed to spark between them, making her skin heat more quickly than if she'd been sitting in the Turkish sun and her lungs to feel squeezed, so that her breath became a little shallow. She ran a finger around the neckline of her dress.

From being two people at odds with one another, determined to keep themselves isolated, she suddenly felt as if they were being pulled towards each other in some magnetic way. She leaned against the back of her chair, but the sun caught her directly in the eyes, around the edge of the shade cloth, and she had to lean forwards again. She wondered if he felt it, or if it was entirely in her own imagination.

Fleetingly, she saw a flash of what she'd seen last night. A look of uncertainty flickered in his eyes, as if he'd thought he knew the answer to something but suddenly doubted himself. She wanted to ask what was bothering him, but hesitated, unsure of how to frame the question. A forceful, independent man like him was not going to admit to any insecurities, to a woman he barely knew.

This had been a mistake. He'd probably only agreed to sit down with her out of politeness. The best thing she could do, for both of them, was leave.

'Where's your bike?'

The question took her by surprise. 'It's leaning against the wall around the corner. Why do you want to know?'

'I can see you're trying to think of how to leave, although I'd like it if you stayed a little longer. Let me wheel it around here for you.'

'Would you?'

'At least finish your tea.'

She peered into the glass, then topped it up. 'It's just...' Beth felt flustered by his intuition. What else about her was so obvious to him? 'I don't like to leave it too late because it'll be hotter for the ride home.'

'Of course.' He inclined his head. His expression was implacable again, showing no trace of emotion.

She drained her glass and pushed her chair back.

Jensen stood and went to get her bike while she slipped her laptop into its bag, put on her sunglasses and dug in her purse for money to pay for her tea.

'Thank you,' she said when he returned. She

put a banknote on the table, dumped her bag in the basket at the front of the bike and took hold of the handlebars. 'I hope you get good advice at the clinic. Let me...' She'd been going to ask him to let her know what happened, but she remembered that they didn't want to see each other.

'Shall I let you know what they say?'

She nodded. 'Yes, please. And...' she drew in a deep breath '...if you need any help, you know where I am.'

'Thank you, Beth.' He smiled, his eyes crinkling at the corners. 'I think I'll be just fine.'

Beth smiled back at him. She watched his long, tanned fingers unwrap themselves from around the handlebars of her bicycle and then his hands disappear into his pockets. She puffed out a long breath. She'd made the offer and it was up to him to decide whether he needed her help or not. She didn't expect to see him again, any time soon, and she'd also be just fine with that.

After all, neither of them wanted to spend time in each other's company.

Jensen watched Beth cycle away, her pink dress billowing around her legs, then he sat down again at the table, taking another piece of baklava in his fingers. Ela appeared in the darkened doorway, and he reached for his wallet, adding the cost of his coffee to the note Beth had left, plus a hefty tip.

If they could keep their encounters brief and light, like last night and this morning, they might enjoy spending a little time together, if she wanted that. He explored the feeling of mild annoyance that came with acknowledging it was what *he* wanted. For months, all he'd wanted was to be alone, to sort out his mind and find answers to the questions that plagued him. He shouldn't want Beth to intrude.

The image of her standing, alone, on the terrace last night had stayed with him. He'd noted that her green dress was a shade or two darker than her eyes. This morning, he might have missed her in the shade outside the café, but she'd stood up and come towards him, with that wide smile, and something inside him, which had been held tight for a long time, had loosened. He didn't understand what it was, but it felt good.

He hadn't thought twice about accepting her invitation to join her.

As he stood up, something beneath the table caught his eye. It was the charger cable for her laptop. He bent to pick it up, turning it over in his hands, looking in the direction of where she'd exited the square in case she'd realised her mistake and come pedalling back.

There was no sign of her, and if she'd kept going, she'd be too far away by now for him to catch up with her on foot. It occurred to Jensen that she wouldn't miss the cable until the next time she needed it.

He coiled the cable up and pushed it into one of his cargo shorts' pockets. He'd visit the clinic, buy his bread and olives, and then head back down to the harbour, where he'd left the RIB tied up at the jetty. Beth would be home by the time he'd motored up the coast back to the cove and climbed the twisting path to the villa. His fist closed around the coiled cable in his pocket. The fact that he felt pleased to have a reason to visit her again was irritating, but he pushed that aside.

Beth left the village behind her and kept pedalling. She tackled a hill at full tilt but had to slow down part way up it. The sun beat down on her bare head and she wished she'd remembered to bring her straw hat.

The day-to-day order of her thoughts and life had encountered a blip. There was something about Jensen, who stood so tall and seemingly steadfast, that kept snagging her attention. Having only recently allowed herself to admit to her own vulnerability, she thought she recognised a stubborn refusal to acknowledge the existence of it in himself. Behind his façade of manly strength and endurance, through the flashes of uncertainty he'd allowed her to glimpse in unguarded moments, she sensed the presence of hurt and confusion.

There was a tentativeness about him, which suggested he held himself in constant expectation of things going wrong.

It takes one to know one, she thought grimly, as she freewheeled down a slope, enjoying the breeze in her face.

She thought back to her confused, bewildered self of two months ago. She might still have a long way to go. After all, she remained homeless and unemployed. But she now had the clarity of thought to recognise how far she had come, and that was what she had to focus on, in order to keep moving forward, with her life, both personal and professional.

Her narrow, restricted existence was in the past. Having the ties that had bound her forcibly cut had been terrifying at the time, and although she didn't know what shape her life would take in the future, at least she was free to make her own decisions.

Something momentous had driven Jensen to sail, single-handed, back to the place where he'd expected to find solitude and solace. Beth wondered if, or when, he'd realise that reaching that goal was only the very beginning of the journey.

She crested the top of a slope and stopped for a breather. A slight breeze at the top of the hill cooled her skin as she enjoyed the glimpses of the sparkling blue sea and the dramatic views of the mountains in the distance.

She set off again, but as she reached the bottom of the hill the bicycle lurched beneath her and pulled to one side of the track. Tugging on the brakes, she skidded to a stop in a cloud of dust. The front wheel was completely flat. Bending to examine it, she found a thorn protruding from the wall of the tyre. She sighed. She'd have to walk the rest of the way, pushing the bike. The hill rising up in front of her was steep and shadeless and she thought she was only about halfway home. The journey, usually enjoyable, was turning into an ordeal.

Pushing a bike with a flat tyre was harder than she'd anticipated. Every stone sent a jolt through the frame and she had to fight to keep going in a reasonably straight line. Her flimsy, rope-soled espadrilles had been designed for wearing to the beach, not for hiking through the harsh Turkish landscape in the almost-midday sun. She could feel the rub of a blister forming on her right heel and a rivulet of sweat trickled down her back, between her shoulder blades.

After several stops to rest, when she tried to regain her breath, she trudged to the crest of the hill. If swimming was going to keep her fit, she'd have to dedicate more time to it. Down in the valley on the far side she could see a single, stunted tree.

The tree provided even less shade than she'd

hoped, but she laid her bicycle on the stony track, making sure that her laptop was safe in the basket, then she sat down on the dusty ground, leaning against the tree trunk. The bark was rough and scratchy against her back.

Her parched mouth and throat longed for a drink of water. Dust coated her feet and legs and the heat intensified as the sun climbed towards its noon-day high point. It was no use berating herself for the position in which she found herself. She should have had a hat and water, but there was nothing she could have done about the punctured tyre.

She'd rest for an hour and then tackle the remainder of the journey.

The phone in her bag was useless. Even if a signal existed out here in the wilds, there was nobody she could call for help. It was a sobering thought.

She closed her eyes, but a rustle in the undergrowth nearby made her shoot bolt upright again, staring at the dry, crackling grass that moved, inches from her right hand. Rigid, she waited, wondering if it was a snake. Not daring to blink and hardly daring to breathe, she shifted slightly further away and watched as a scaley, blunt-nosed head appeared, swinging from side to side. Then she breathed out as a small tortoise, leathery neck stretched from its bumpy shell, emerged from the scrub. Ignoring her, it lumbered its slow, measured way across the track.

Beth rested her head against the tree trunk and prepared to wait.

CHAPTER FIVE

THE BOTTOM OF the RIB scraped on the shingle as Jensen beached the craft. He climbed out, pulled it further out of the water and looked around.

He'd wondered if Beth, knowing he was in the village, might have come down for a swim. But the heat was scorching, and he thought she was probably resting in the shade of her terrace, enjoying a siesta.

It was already mid-afternoon. After a long wait at the clinic, buying food and water and making the journey back to *Sundance*, he was later than he'd expected to be.

There was no trace of Beth at the villa, either. The sun lounger was empty, and the sliding glass doors were locked. He circled around the house and tried the front door. The door to the lean-to storeroom was open, and he looked in, seeing a beach volleyball net, two paddle boards but no bicycle.

A finger of disquiet traced up Jensen's spine and he rattled the brass handle of the front door again. The silence in the oppressive afternoon heat suddenly felt unnatural. Beth should have been home long ago.

He stepped back, getting his bearings. He could remember vaguely, from before the villa had been built, where the track began, and he soon found it, winding downhill into the trees. He was pleased that he was wearing his boat shoes. They might be battered, but they would provide a good grip on the rough surface.

As he stepped into the trees he heard a mechanical squeak, and the sound of stones on the track being dislodged. He paused to listen and heard irregular footsteps and uneven breathing from below him.

Beth came into view, rounding a bend in the track. She was pushing her bicycle, limping and her cheeks were as pink as the dress she wore. She stopped, swiped a forearm across her forehead and blew out a long breath, looking up at the final slope ahead of her.

'Jensen?'

He started down towards her. 'What's happened? Are you all right?'

'What are you doing here?'

'Looking for you.'

'Why? We aren't supposed to want to see each other.'

Jensen took the bike from her. 'Let me do this. You're limping.'

Beth let go of the bike and wiped her palms across her face. 'The front tyre has a thorn in it. Pushing a bike with a flat tyre is hard work.' She looked up the hill. 'Almost there. And it's only a blister.' She grimaced. 'A big blister.'

'Have you got water with you?'

She shook her head. Tendrils that had escaped from the knot of her hair flew around her face.

'I forgot to bring my water bottle.' She planted her fists on her hips. 'And my hat.'

'That was...'

'Stupid. Yes, I know.'

'I was going to say "unfortunate".'

'I don't forget things. Not usually.'

'I'll take the bike.'

Beth nodded. 'Thank you.'

They emerged from the trees into the glare of the afternoon sun and Jensen bumped the bike across the dry grass towards the house. 'Get yourself a drink of water. You may feel like swallowing a gallon, but take a few sips, at first. Otherwise you may feel sick.' He wheeled the bike into the storeroom.

When he went into the house she was in the kitchen, a glass of water in her hand.

'You haven't told me why you're here.'

He put the bag containing her laptop on the kitchen island and pulled the charging cable from his pocket. 'You dropped this under that table at the café.'

'Ah. Thank you. I'd probably have thought I'd dropped it on the track somewhere. I'd have retraced my steps, looking for it. Not an attractive idea, right now.' She sipped from the glass. 'How was the clinic?' She limped across the floor and slid open the glass doors onto the terrace.

'I've been given meds for what seems to be a mild infection.' He looked down at Beth's feet. 'There's blood on the heel of your shoe.'

'I know. I've tried to take it off, but it's stuck.' She kicked off the other espadrille. 'I'll have to soak it in water.'

'Do you need help?'

She shook her head. 'No, thank you. I might have to grit my teeth, but I'll manage.'

'I'll have a look for a puncture repair kit in the storeroom while you do that.'

She turned quickly to face him. 'Will you be able to mend the tyre if you find one?'

He nodded. 'Sailing teaches you to be handy and resourceful. If I can't mend it, I'll take the wheel to the village in the RIB tomorrow. Someone there will be able to do it.'

'That will cause you even more trouble than I have already.'

He folded his arms and regarded her steadily. 'Maybe, but what will you do the next time you need to get to Sula? It's almost too difficult for you to ride, in this heat. It's definitely too far to walk.' He glanced down at her feet. 'Especially with an injured foot.'

'I'm resourceful, too. I'll think of something.' She returned to the kitchen and pulled a plastic bowl from a cupboard, filling it with water.

Her back was poker-straight as she limped across the tiled floor and into the spacious, open-plan living area. Deep sofas, covered in cream linen, were grouped around a low, marble-topped table, facing the terrace and pool through a wall of glass. At one end of the room the up-to-date kitchen gleamed with porcelain tiles and polished appliances. Cool white walls and cream curtains pulled the scheme together, creating a room that combined elegance and charm with a laid-back informality.

Over to the left, Jensen noticed a wide, open fireplace in the end wall. The idea of a log fire when the mercury was climbing towards forty degrees seemed like madness, but he knew how cold it would be here in the depths of winter, when icy winds from distant, snow-covered mountain peaks in the north roared over the headlands.

The presence of this villa intruded on his solitude and spoiled his memories. He wished the land had been left wild and undeveloped. But he had to admit, unwillingly, that if he had designed it, this was exactly how he would have wanted it to be.

If the villa weren't here, Beth wouldn't be here

either. Would that have been the perfect scenario he'd dreamt about? It didn't feel so attractive anymore. Being with her somehow soothed him. The knots of tension he'd carried for months seemed to unravel a little. It shouldn't be like this, he told himself, watching her sit on the sofa and lower her injured heel into the bowl of water. He should be on *Sundance*, grappling with how he was going to find some sort of life for himself.

Was that what Beth was doing, too?

CHAPTER SIX

BETH EASED THE shoe away from the injury on her heel. The skin was raw and red. As she stood up, Jensen walked back into the room.

'I can repair the tyre. I've found a kit in the store.' He bent his head to peer at her heel. 'How's the blister?'

'Thank you. I'd really appreciate that. And the blister is not great. I need to put a dressing on it.'

'Is there a first-aid kit in the house?'

'Under the sink, I think.' She eased herself back onto the sofa. 'Could you get it?'

Jensen carried the box across the room and put it on the marble table in front of her.

'Can you manage? It looks a little nasty.'

Beth laughed. 'I think I can deal with my own blister but thank you for offering.' She heard the rasp of his palm as he pulled it across his jaw, and she looked up. 'I'm used to taking care of myself.'

'Maybe, but that doesn't mean you can never accept help.' Jensen took a step back, away from her. 'I know your privacy is important to you. You didn't ask me in. I followed you, so I should go. The walk must have tired you out.'

Beth shook her head and a tendril of hair escaped from its untidy knot and flopped forward over her forehead. She pushed it back. 'I think I might be too much of a coward to put on the antiseptic.'

'If I'd found you sooner, I wouldn't have let you walk.' He nodded towards her foot. 'I would have loaded you onto the bike and pushed you all the way home.'

'I would have resisted, for sure.'

Beth took a tube of antiseptic and a pad of cottonwool from the first-aid box. Frowning and biting her lip, she returned her attention to her heel.

'Shall I do that? It's a slightly awkward angle for you. If you turn around I'll be better able to see your heel.'

'Would you? Thank you.' Beth shifted her position, turning towards the back of the sofa to expose her heel and resting her head on her folded arms. 'Are you a doctor?' she asked suddenly, looking back over her shoulder at him.

'No, I'm not. Why do you ask?'

Beth turned her face away again. 'Injuries don't seem to bother you.'

'Like I said earlier, sailing means having to develop all sorts of skills. I've dealt with way worse things than this, sometimes in the teeth of a gale, on high seas, at night.'

'Really? Like what?'

'Oh, fingers trapped in winches, heads smacked by the boom whipping across unexpectedly, twisted ankles...'

'It sounds like a violent pastime. Ow!'

'Sorry. Almost done now. I'll put a dressing on it but you're going to have to keep it dry for a couple of days.'

The crackling rip of an Elastoplast dressing being unwrapped sounded loud in the quiet room. He pressed it to the back of her heel and removed his hands.

Beth hadn't been at all sure she'd be able to bear having him touch her foot, but his calm ministrations and matter-of-fact manner had made her forget the way she shrank from contact these days.

She had no memory of straightforward affection. Her mother was a vague shadow who had faded away before Beth's memories of her had been properly formed. She thought her father had remarried quickly to try to replace her, both for himself and for his small daughter. If he'd ever regretted it, he had never said. He seemed to shrink in her memory, after that, and the figure of her stepmother and then her baby half-sister grew large and overwhelming. Physical displays of affection or words of praise became forbidden.

It had been years before Beth had realised that not all families behaved in that way. She had felt like an intruder in her own home, an unwanted member of her own family. When she hadn't felt invisible, she'd been criticised. Her hair was unruly. It must always be kept tied back, tightly. Bright colours did not suit her. The clothes bought for her were dull and unflattering. She'd grown into a young woman who believed herself to be unattractive.

Later, her usefulness had been in working hard to keep the household running. It had only been after the death of her stepmother that she'd learned there hadn't been a shortage of money. She could have gone on to study botany and horticulture if her stepmother had allowed it.

And then, although her father had extracted a verbal promise from his wife to leave the house in Islington to her, she'd left it to her own daughter instead, who intended to sell it, depriving Beth of the home she'd had since birth.

She twisted round and pulled her feet up under the skirt of her dress, hugging her knees. Jensen's dark head was bent over the first-aid box, those long fingers reordering the contents, clicking the lid shut, folding the cloth and towel.

'That means no swimming.' She frowned. 'I'll have to do more gardening, in the early mornings. And I'll have to cycle into the village for entertainment and exercise.'

'I wouldn't put a closed shoe on until the skin has healed, or you'll risk rubbing it raw again. And I wouldn't advise cycling in flip-flops.'

'Not that I have to listen to your advice.'

'No, you don't.' He shrugged.

His easy response surprised her. All the men she'd worked for had assumed that their opinions should be accepted without challenge.

What would working for Jensen be like? she wondered. Was he as calm and considerate in the workplace as he'd been when applying a dressing to her blistered heel? He gave the impression of being a good leader; one who would use quiet example rather than unreasonable demands. Beneath his measured exterior must lie a fierce determination, though, and an expectation of being obeyed, if he could command the respect and obedience of a crew at sea in dangerous conditions.

What had brought him to this remote part of the Turkish coast, alone?

'Is that what you do?' As soon as she'd spoken, Beth realised her words would have no context for him. She had become so familiar with her own internal monologue she'd forgotten that she hadn't spoken it out loud.

Jensen moved to the nearby armchair. 'Do what?' The lines between his eyes deepened. He propped his folded arms across his knees and turned his head to look at her.

'Sorry. I...was wondering what you do. From what you say, you're used to sailing with a crew.' She pressed her face to her knees, before looking across at him. 'I apologise. It's nothing to do with me. I just thought you might be a professional sailor.'

'For me, sailing is purely recreational. And therapeutic. It's not a job. It's an indulgence.' He tapped his fingertips on the marble table. 'Sailing alone is the perfect way to banish everyday worries, and even bigger ones. The level of concentration needed is intense. It eclipses everything else.'

'But you're not sailing now. You're anchored in the cove, going nowhere.'

A thrumming silence stretched between them.

'That's because...' He took a big breath. 'It's because things have happened in my life which I need to address,' he eventually said, slowly. 'For a long time, I dreamed of getting back here. It felt as if only here would I find the space and the silence I needed to sort things out. Not just physical space and silence. I suppose peace and headspace would describe it best. But...'

'But you finally arrived, only to find me—and the villa—here, in your special place.'

He sat back, clasping his hands behind his head, balancing an ankle on a knee. 'Yes, but I think I'm discovering that...you...are not really the problem.'

Beth smiled. 'Always good to know I'm not a problem. But if it's not me?'

He turned his head away, looking out through the glass doors towards the pool and the trees. 'This may sound crazy...' He shook his head. 'I don't know if you'll understand.'

Beth saw that self-doubt take hold again in his dark eyes. She thought back to the person she'd been when she'd first arrived in Turkey, weeks ago. She'd felt hollowed out, invisible. Sure that nobody needed her and certain that nobody wanted her. Her childhood home and precious garden were being sold and she'd walked away from the job that had given her identity and purpose for twenty-five years. It had been the place where she felt she belonged, and, lately, was appreciated for herself, rather than her organisational ability.

For days, she'd wanted to stay curled up in bed, the air conditioning blowing cold, the blinds keeping out the hot Turkish summer. But hunger had drawn her out, and each time she'd ventured into the bright living space downstairs, the outdoors she could see through the wide glass doors had worked a little more of its magic on her. Bright birds had swooped over the pool and congregated in the rosemary bushes that grew wild along the edge of the terrace. A striped lizard had blinked slowly, its head raised, basking in the sun.

One day, she'd slid open the doors and felt the warm, dry air brush against her face, and the scent of the grass and pine trees tickle her nostrils. Janet's voice had come to her, so clearly that she'd almost looked over her shoulder, expecting to see her standing inside the front door.

'The house will stand empty if you don't go and live in it. You'll be doing us a favour.'

'I can't accept it. It makes me feel like a hopeless case. Homeless and unemployed.'

'If you go and live there you won't be homeless. And you can use the time to search for another—a *better*—job. And if you still feel you owe us, please use your horticultural skills and do something about getting the garden started. Omer, Emin's cousin, will tell you where to get plants in Sula.'

It had been a slow process, but from that moment she'd had a purpose.

'You could try me, Jensen. You never know. I might just understand.'

He seemed to pull himself back into the room from somewhere distant. A frown, almost of puzzlement, creased his forehead and drew his brows together. His eyes, filled with doubt, found hers.

'The journey was tough, sometimes. But I liked those times best. I felt powerful, managing the boat, reading the weather, trying to predict the waves. There was no one else to rely on. Just me. I had to keep control, of everything, because disaster was always waiting to strike if I let my attention stray.'

Beth nodded. 'It sounds frightening.'

'It would have been if I'd allowed fear into my head. But I refused. Fear is corrosive. I thought I'd won the battle before I even reached the destination where I'd intended to fight it.'

'Here?'

He nodded. 'Here.'

Beth tucked her legs up onto the sofa and smoothed the skirt of her dress over her feet. 'And when you arrived...'

'It took a day or two, but then I found it wasn't like I thought it would be. I'd reached my goal. I'd stopped, at last, and could relax and think about what to do.'

'But?'

'But I can't relax and I can't think. That power I thought I had was an illusion. I could control *Sundance*, use my knowledge to make the best of the wind and the weather, but I cannot control my thoughts or my emotions. I'm confused and doubtful that I'll ever sort things out. And most of all, I hate the idea that this might all have been for nothing.'

'I don't think,' Beth said, carefully, 'that anything is for nothing. Things happen for a reason. You may not be able to see the reason yet, but you will eventually. When I first came here, I had lost all purpose. My life had spun out of control, and it felt as if everything I'd ever known or valued had been snatched away.'

'What happened?'

She shook her head. 'Knowing that wouldn't help you, Jensen. Just as knowing what has brought you here is irrelevant to me. What I discovered is that reaching the destination is only the beginning. The journey is still ahead of you. It may seem impossibly difficult, and you may not know where it's leading, but if you take one day at a time, you'll get there.'

Jensen rubbed a hand over the back of his neck. She kept her eyes on his face and he met her gaze with his own. She smiled at him.

'Thank you, Beth. I thought I wanted solitude but talking to you helps to put things into some sort of perspective. I didn't think I'd be able to say this, but I don't mind the villa, with you in it, nearly as much as I did.'

An unfamiliar mix of emotions stirred behind her breastbone. Muted pleasure, at his words, and satisfaction that her own experience, to date, might have helped him a little. And something else: a faint frisson of anticipation of the beginning of a tentative friendship between them.

'I've taken up most of your day, Jensen. Thank you for your help'.

'You're welcome, Beth. I was pleased to help, even though you denied needing it, and I've enjoyed your company.'

Silence stretched between them, but it was companionable and comfortable. Beth felt it could be left like that. They didn't need to fill it with words.

He'd said he didn't mind her being here. That did not mean they were going to become new best friends.

She pressed her bare feet to the cool tiles and stood up, walking to the glass doors, keeping her back to him. 'You've been very kind and I owe you thanks.' She inhaled a deep breath, trying to control the tremor in her voice, which would give away how anxious she was for him to accept what she said next. 'I'll owe you even more thanks if you repair the puncture. May I cook dinner for you tomorrow as a thank you?'

CHAPTER SEVEN

BETH HAD TRIED to keep her voice steady. He could tell that by her straight spine and pulled-back shoulders, but she hadn't quite managed it. It reminded him that, while she might look and sound strong and positive, there was a vulnerability beneath the façade she was presenting to the world.

He stood up and moved to stand next to her at the glass doors. 'I wouldn't be comfortable accepting your invitation if your only reason for issuing it is to discharge a debt of gratitude.' He cast a quick sideways glance at her profile, noticing her chin lifting in something like defiance. Or perhaps it was self-defence. She opened her mouth, about to reply, but he held up a hand. 'If, on the other hand, your invitation is to share a meal with me and perhaps enjoy my company as well, then...'

She turned abruptly towards him, her hands clasped together, her gaze direct.

'I've been on my own, here, for weeks. I've

never socialised much, but now I'm well and truly out of the habit.'

He nodded, filing that information away to examine another time. 'I'm not much different. I was pleased to help you today, but I don't need repayment, of any sort.' He stepped away from her, aware of the tension radiating from her body. 'I'll get on with fixing your bike.'

He could mend the tyre and walk away from Beth—from this unsettling need to spend more time with her; to try to find out more about her—and return to the solitude of *Sundance*'s deck.

That seemed to be what she wanted, and he was not going to push her for reasons.

He worked methodically, completing the repair and re-inflating the tyre. With the bike returned to its place on a rack in the store, he packed away the tools he'd used and emerged into the late afternoon sunlight.

Beth stood on the rough grass, pink flip-flops on her feet.

'Before you use the bike again check that the tyre is still properly inflated.'

'Jensen?'

He'd been about to walk away, but he stopped. 'Yes?'

'Thank you. But…'

'But you don't want my company. That's fine, Beth.'

'That's not what I was going to say.' She lifted

her hands, palms upwards. 'What I mean is, I've enjoyed your company, too, and I think I could enjoy more of it.'

He smiled at her, keeping his distance.

'You think? What,' he asked, 'are the chances of you finding out for sure? One in ten? In fifty?'

'No chances,' she replied. 'I've decided. I'd like you to come for dinner. That is, if you don't already have a dinner party planned on *Sundance* tomorrow evening.'

He shook his head, welcoming the glimpse of humour that sparkled in her eyes. 'No, I don't. I just happen to be free.'

'Good. Would seven o'clock suit you? It'll probably be pasta.'

'Excellent. I'll bring a bottle of wine.'

'Does that mean you have to go back to the village tomorrow?'

'I'll raid the cellar on *Sundance*.'

'You have a cellar on *Sundance*? Is that ballast?'

'It could be if the need arose. And it's not really a cellar, obviously. It's a few bottles of wine wedged into the cubby holes above the main berth.'

Yesterday, this had seemed like a good idea. She'd enjoyed Jensen's company and was grateful for his help in mending her bike and dressing her blistered heel. The awareness that had sparked between them at the little café table had faded by the afternoon, she thought, allowing her space to begin to relax in his company. With that had come the realisation that perhaps he might need help in confronting whatever demons had brought him here.

She had no idea what those might be, but she could listen, if he wanted to talk.

Why, then, when she'd woken from a restless night, had inviting him to dinner seemed like the worst idea in the world?

Beth turned off the shower, wrapped a towel around herself, and thought about the contents of her wardrobe, wondering what to wear, then reminded herself that she was cooking a simple supper of pasta, not a four-course dinner party with four different bottles of wine. Stressing over her outfit was not necessary.

She pulled on a pair of cream linen crops and a loose-fitting top with elbow-length sleeves. Before stepping into the shower, she'd made a sauce from the fresh tomatoes, peppers, garlic and onions she'd had in the fridge, adding a few sprigs of herbs from the pots she'd planted up around the terrace. A rich aroma now floated up the stairs.

She rubbed condensation off the surface of the mirror and studied her reflection. She'd caught the sun the previous day, on her long walk from Sula, and her cheeks glowed more than she'd have liked. Jensen had made it plain that friendship was what he sought, so the nerves jumping in her tummy were ridiculous and annoying. It was, she told herself, because she hadn't cooked a meal for anyone other than herself, for months. Her skills as a hostess were non-existent.

Why had she done this to herself? It hadn't been necessary to put herself under stress.

Then she reminded herself how far she'd come in the past few weeks. Certain things might still make her anxious, but serving pasta and tomato sauce to one other person should not be one of them. It wasn't as if she planned to bare her soul to him. Her heart and soul were carefully locked away, where they couldn't be damaged any more than they had been already.

Get a grip, she told her reflection, already blurred by more condensation.

A slick of lip gloss took away the dryness that over-exposure to the sun had caused, and she towelled her hair vigorously before blow-drying it roughly and reaching for a scrunchie. As the whine of the dryer died away, she heard the knock on the door. Her stomach plunged. Of course he was early, and she wasn't ready.

'Beth?'

Why hadn't she locked the door?

'Beth?' His voice was steady, calm, coming from the foot of the stairs. 'Are you okay?'

Beth dropped the scrunchie and combed her fingers through her hair, trying to tidy it into vague orderliness, as she walked down the short passage to the curving staircase, knowing that curls would be falling around her shoulders in an unruly mass. Too bad. This wasn't a work dinner. She didn't have to entertain an important client. This was the wild Turkish coast and she wasn't obliged to look perfectly groomed.

The marble floor was cool beneath her bare feet, her footsteps silent. She rounded the curve in the flight of steps and found Jensen looking up at her.

She decided, again, that this had been a bad idea. Her fingers tightened on the iron railing that curved up around the stairs. He looked cool and fresh, his hair slicked back, his navy eyes calm. Not at all as if his appearance had just delivered a potent kick to her abdomen.

'Hey.'

'Hello. You're...'

'I'm a little early. I apologise.'

'I wasn't quite ready.' She lifted the hand that wasn't gripping the banister and ran it over her hair.

'Something in the kitchen smells delicious.'

He had swapped his shorts and faded tee shirt from yesterday for jeans and a pale blue shirt, slightly crumpled, open at the throat and with the sleeves rolled to the elbows. She wished she felt as relaxed as he looked, a bottle of wine in one hand, the other in the pocket of his jeans.

'Oh,' she said, 'thank you,' wondering again

what had made her do this. Perhaps if she'd put her hair up she would have felt more in control of the situation. Of *herself.* A sleek French pleat was the image she liked to present to the world: severe, remote.

Don't even think of crossing my personal boundary.

'Your hair looks beautiful.'

'Beautiful?'

'Yes,' he said. 'Beautiful. Now, I don't know about you, but I'm hungry and thirsty and this bottle of wine won't open itself.'

She didn't understand why she felt so anxious about this evening. It should have been so simple. She took a deep breath to steady herself so that she could at least walk down the stairs towards him without wobbling, but she needn't have worried. He'd turned away and was strolling towards the kitchen.

Beth had a sudden, vivid flashback to her old life, where chairing a meeting or arranging a client dinner had been something she did every day, without a second thought. What had become of that version of herself? It had vanished the day she'd walked out of the office, her reason for being taken away from her and the future she'd imagined in tatters.

She blocked the memory and made herself think, instead, of how a sense of purpose and self-worth had begun to creep back into her consciousness when she'd decided to start planning Janet's garden and nurturing the plants she'd bought for it.

Jensen's dark, steady gaze seemed to be able to see into her, beyond the image she presented to the outside world, to question things about her that she'd rather keep secret. He made her feel vulnerable again because he made her...*feel*.

She didn't want to return to that sort of feeling. She'd had enough of the cold weight of shock and devastating hurt that lodged in her stomach whenever she allowed herself to think about the turn her life had taken. Being surrounded by the peace and beauty of this place had enabled her to keep those damaging emotions under control, choosing when and where to examine them. She knew she had to examine them, in order to move on, but it had to be done at her own pace, when the time was right. No longer, she thought, did she sometimes have to fold an arm across her abdomen, giving in to the sensation that it was the only way to keep herself together.

Jensen was opening drawers in the kitchen, humming under his breath. No doubt he was searching for a corkscrew.

Shaking her hair out over her shoulders—had he really said it looked beautiful?—she filled her lungs, exhaled strongly, straightened her spine and walked down the stairs, putting on her formal, PA face. It was her best defence and, under these circumstances, her only weapon.

Jensen located a complicated corkscrew in the second drawer he opened. He sliced around the foil covering the cork and peeled it away, positioning the device over the top of the bottle. Then he looked up and saw Beth coming towards him.

He breathed a quiet sigh of relief. He'd had the feeling she'd had second thoughts about this evening and wanted to disappear upstairs, but he wasn't at all sure what he would have done about it if she had. He couldn't have gone after her. He could have waited, hoping she might change her mind or offer an explanation, but he might have waited a long time.

Her rigid posture made her movements jerky and he saw the tip of her tongue run quickly across her lower lip. Suddenly and inappropriately, he imagined how her soft mouth would feel beneath the rough pad of his thumb.

She looked ready to shatter into a thousand sharp pieces of herself. He did not want to be the catalyst for that event. He wanted her to feel comfortable.

He smiled, hoping that it looked easy, and that Beth wouldn't notice the tension he felt. 'Could you find some glasses?'

'I don't want...'

He paused in what he was doing. 'I'm sorry.

It was presumptive of me to assume you'd want wine. What else have you got? Would you prefer something soft?'

'No. No, thank you.'

She stopped on the far side of the marble-topped kitchen island. The pale green colour of her loose-fitting top was the perfect foil for her eyes, he thought. And her hair really was beautiful, with its streaks of faded gold threading through darker amber. But her expression bordered on fierce, faint lines creasing the wide space between her brows.

He forced himself to take his eyes off her and go back to opening the bottle, working slowly, twisting the metal screw into the cork and pressing down on the two levers to remove it smoothly, with a muted, satisfying pop.

He glanced round the kitchen and saw glasses lined up in neat rows on shelves. 'Ah, there they are. Sure you won't have wine?' He squinted at the label. 'I bought it on a sailing trip in the South of France a couple of years ago. I've been waiting for an occasion to try it.'

At last, Beth nodded. 'Thank you. I'd like some.'

Jensen decided not to ask her what she'd been going to say. He didn't understand what had happened to make her so nervous, but probing would only make it worse. He selected two stemmed goblets and set them on the marble countertop, pouring the golden wine from the bottle.

He held a glass out to Beth, noticing the slight

tremor of her hand as she took it. 'Shall we sit on the terrace? It's a little cooler now.' Perhaps she'd feel more relaxed on the terrace.

Without waiting for an answer, Jensen slid the glass doors open and stood back, allowing Beth to go ahead of him. The air was warm with no hint of a breeze. The cicadas, which had been in full cry in the earlier heat, had fallen silent and in the west the sky still held the pink glow of sunset. Soft pools of light from concealed solar lanterns glowed in the garden. Two candle lanterns stood unlit on the wooden table.

'There're matches in the kitchen.' Beth turned back into the house, colliding with him as he stepped through the door. He put his free hand on her shoulder, to steady her, but she jerked away from him.

The connection between them lasted only a few seconds but it was long enough for Jensen to feel, not only the softness of her body against him, but also the taut muscles of her upper arm beneath his hand. He caught the floral scent of shampoo, the clean smell of soap. How easy it would be, he thought, to slide his hand down around her waist and hold her against him for a little longer. How easy, but how impossible.

Even if she'd been willing to give him a quick hug, was that what he wanted? He didn't think so. Beth intrigued him. She was complicated and prickly and that combination piqued his interest, but friendship was the only thing he was prepared to offer her, or any other woman, right now, so if there was one thing he was hell-bent on doing, it was keeping a lid on the sensations that fired into unwelcome life whenever she was near. A hug, however brief and friendly, would not be helpful.

She returned with a box of matches. The quick scrape of the match head against the side of the box sounded loud in the silence. The small orange flame flared and she leaned over the table, lifting the glass chimney of one of the lamps and lighting the candle. The wick caught, sending up a tall lick of dancing flame, before settling into a steady burn, light pooling around it on the table.

'Thank you for inviting me.' He raised his glass and she nodded, doing the same, and then taking a mouthful of the honey-coloured wine. 'I don't have to stay long.'

She almost smiled and he thought that somehow what he'd said had ticked a mental box for her. Was she pleased he wouldn't stay long? Or had she told herself he'd eat and be gone?

'This wine is exceptional. Thank you.' She put her glass on the table. 'I'll put the pasta on.'

Beth reminded herself how easy she'd found his company the day before. The best way to get through the evening was to try to recapture that feeling of relaxed companionship between them. The fact that the silence felt charged and awkward was entirely her fault. She'd used up all her reserves of emotional energy preparing for him to be here and now she had none left for making conversation.

Frustration bloomed inside her. Why couldn't she relax and enjoy the evening for what it was? Two people, possibly both lonely, sharing simple food and finding pleasure in each other's company. She couldn't relax because she was afraid of the emotions that might escape from the locked-down state in which she kept them. She couldn't afford to drop her guard. She never would, again.

'How is your heel?' Jensen had pushed his cleaned plate aside and now sat, leaning his folded arms on the table.

This was safe territory, Beth thought. Her heel was the reason he was here at all.

'It feels good, thank you.' She nodded, smiling. 'I've washed my shoes and they'll be wearable again.'

'Just don't put them on before the skin has healed completely.'

'I won't, but staying out of the water for a day or two is going to be a challenge.' She reached for his plate, stacking it on top of her own. 'How is your leg?'

'Definitely improving. Twenty-four hours on the antibiotic and I can tell it's going to be fine.'

'Luckily I haven't needed to use the clinic but it's good to know there is one.'

'That was delicious. Thank you. Who taught you to cook?' He took a mouthful of wine, watching her over the rim of the glass.

'Oh, I'm self-taught,' she replied. As far as safe topics of conversation went, cooking must surely come second only to the weather. She could move on to the midday temperatures and strength of the breeze, when there was one, if the conversation flagged.

'You mean you didn't have an Italian grandmother or aunt, teaching you the wizardry of combining ingredients, from an early age?'

'No grandmother, or aunt.' She took the paper napkin from her lap and folded it in half on the table, smoothing the crease with her thumb.

'None at all? Italian or otherwise?'

She shook her head. 'None.' In the silence that followed she folded the paper oblong she'd created into a square. Perhaps now was the moment to comment on the brightness of the stars, or the lack of light pollution.

But she'd reckoned without Jensen.

'Did you teach yourself to cook, Beth? Was it something that interested you?'

Beth thought of the years she'd spent planning and shopping for economical and nutritious meals for her stepmother and half-sister, cooking when she'd come home from a hard day at work to find they hadn't washed up their breakfast dishes. And then discovering she'd been duped and none of it had been necessary. Her father had left a lot of money, just not to her. He had simply been manipulated by the woman he'd married and had been too weak to stand up to her. And then, when circumstances had set her free, and a beautiful, exciting future had seemed to be within her grasp, it had all come crashing down.

'No,' she replied, slowly, picking up her glass and swirling the dregs of wine in it. 'I didn't particularly want to do it. In fact, now I wonder why I did. I could have just walked away, if I hadn't promised my father...'

That was one of the problems of living alone. Sometimes she talked to herself, and this was one of those times. Was she losing her grip on reality? What had she said? Too much, probably. She tipped up the glass and swallowed the last few drops. Jensen stretched an arm across the table and held up the bottle, raising his eyebrows. Recklessly, she allowed him to top up her glass.

'What did you promise your father?'

'My life story is rather dull. You said you didn't want to stay long, so don't feel—'

'That's not what I said at all. I said I didn't *have* to stay long. Not that I didn't want to. And you've told me just enough of a story to keep me interested.'

Beth kept her eyes down, looking at her replenished glass. Did it matter if she told him what had happened? It wouldn't count as baring her soul.

Once they went their separate ways they were never going to see each other again and he'd forget about her, and her sad story as soon as he'd sailed *Sundance* out between the headlands.

She could clam up, but that would lead to more glaring gaps in the conversation. It would be easier to fill them with the irrelevant details of her background. It might also keep Jensen happy. There were questions about her personal life that she would not be happy to answer.

'My father died of cancer when I was sixteen. He asked me to look after my stepmother, Ava, and half-sister.' She raised her glass and took a sip of wine. 'He'd always said the house would be mine, but he changed his will a few days before he passed away. I'd promised to care for them as he seemed to think they were incapable of caring for themselves. I soon discovered that absolutely wasn't true.' She looked across the table to find Jensen's dark eyes on her face.

'Is that when you could have walked away?'

Beth shook her head. 'No. I was still at school, but soon I was running the household, on the limited funds I was allowed. Ava said my father had left very little money to live on but if I fulfilled my promise, she'd told him she'd bequeath the house to me, as he wouldn't ever want me to be without a home.'

'And that didn't happen.'

'No. I eventually became Ava's main carer,

as well as working full-time. When she died a few months ago, she left the house to Sherri, my half-sister. She's ten years younger than me.' She paused, sitting back in her chair. 'You could say I was easily manipulated, but I'd tried to please my father all my life and I continued after he'd died, keeping my promise to care for his wife and daughter. I think he remarried quickly, after my mother died, because he wanted to replace her, both for himself and for me, and eventually Sherri came along, the baby sister I'd always longed for.'

'Only it wasn't like he imagined?'

'Or like I did. His new wife—my new mother—for whom I was meant to be grateful, never intended to be a mother to me, but I had to do a lot of growing up before I realised that. When I left school she told me there was no money for me to go to university.'

She watched as Jensen raised his glass, then replaced it on the table without drinking from it.

'What did you hope to study?'

'Botany and horticulture. I wanted to be a landscape designer. The garden in Islington…' She swallowed a mouthful of wine. 'Well, it was my escape, in a way, when I had the time.'

'So what did you do instead?'

'I went to secretarial college and got my job. I don't know why I'm telling you this. You can't be remotely interested, but that was when I could have walked away.'

He shook his head. 'Don't assume you're not interesting. Was that the job you had until...?'

'I worked for the same company until I...left, a few weeks before coming here.' She noticed that the moon, a perfect crescent, had risen over the trees, wisps of cloud trailing across its face. 'My father was foolish,' she said, steering the conversation away from the subject of her former job. 'He should have tied things up more tightly, legally. I just assumed he had, but I think he changed his will under duress and there was nothing legal to say the house would eventually be left to me.' She shook her head. 'I prefer to believe he would not knowingly have left me without a home.' She saw the muscles of Jensen's jaw tighten, even under his stubble, and his eyes narrowed. 'When Ava died, I discovered there'd been a lot of money in my father's estate. I could have studied further. There'd always seemed to be enough when Sherri needed something.'

'What's she doing now?'

Beth pressed her fingers to her temples, shaking her head. 'She became a successful estate agent in London. After her mother died, she told me she was moving in with her fiancé and selling the house.' She heard Jensen suck in a long, controlled breath.

'Your stepmother's behaviour was outrageous and dishonest.'

'Maybe, but not illegal, and Sherri has promised me a percentage of the value of the sale. There was nothing I could do to stop it. Janet and Emin lending me this house has been a life-saver. Being somewhere so different, away from all my familiar routines, has meant I can be more detached from what happened.' She looked out at the darkened garden. 'And making a garden here for them has been my motivation for keeping going, sometimes. They refused to let me pay rent, but Janet said if I wanted to repay them in some way, I could design the garden. It's what I've been doing today.' She didn't say she'd worked herself to a standstill, in the heat, digging, weeding and planting. It was how she'd kept her anxiety about cooking him dinner at bay.

'Where have you bought the plants? I noticed the newly planted pomegranate yesterday.'

'Omer, at the shop, told me where to get them. There's a small nursery on the outskirts of Sula. He delivered them for me, in his van.' She smiled. 'I couldn't manage more than a few pots of herbs and pelargoniums in the basket of the bike. I was defeated by the pomegranate sapling.'

'And your job, which you'd worked so hard at for so many years?'

Beth met his eyes across the table. His stare was searching, intense, but she was done with sharing. The memories of that awful day were still too recent, too *raw*. She cringed when she remembered how she'd walked to work that morning, feeling as if she were floating on a cloud of happiness. Sherri's announcement that she was selling the house had shocked her at first, but then she'd seen the possibilities it opened up. She'd been freed, by Ava's death and Sherri's decision. When Charles heard what had happened, surely he'd immediately suggest moving in together. She'd resign, find another job, and the secret of their relationship, which she'd hugged to herself for a year, could be made public. They'd be a proper couple. At last, she could plan for the future she craved: a home shared with someone she loved. Someone who loved her back.

Afterwards, she'd wondered if anyone had guessed the truth about them. Who had watched her breeze into the office that day, alight with happy expectation, only to leave again, two hours later, her face streaked with tears? Had there been gossip? Emails flying around the office, speculating?

She'd become anxious about interacting with anyone, never knowing who might be judging her or ridiculing her behind her back. The foundation on which her life had been built for twenty-five years had crumbled, leaving her free-falling through life.

She lifted her chin, stopping her destructive train of thought. 'I don't want to talk about that. I judged something badly. *Very* badly. I paid the price and I…left.'

'You mean you were fired?'

'No. I left. I was in an impossible situation. I couldn't have continued to work there, afterwards.' She watched him frown and look down at the table, rubbing at a mark on the wood with an index finger.

'Were you properly compensated? I could investigate it for you, if you like. Not now, but some time.'

Beth stared at him. 'I know you're not a doctor. Are you a lawyer?'

Jensen shook his head. 'I've retired from all my roles, but that doesn't mean I can't investigate something privately. At some point.'

'That's very generous. I've saved carefully over the years and with some money from the house I'll be able to take a little time about finding another job and somewhere to live. But even so, I couldn't afford to pay you and I don't think a supper of pasta and tomato sauce would cover it, somehow.' She pulled her bare feet up onto the edge of her chair and hugged her shins. 'And anyway, I've taken control of my own life now. It was controlled by others for so long, and I include my work in that. But even though I've lost the anchors that kept me grounded, I'm learning to appreciate the freedom that has given me.' She rested her chin on her knees. 'It has taken weeks, but I'm gradually finding a kind of acceptance of my new state. The future I thought I had planned no longer exists, but that doesn't mean I can't plan a different one. One thing I know for certain is that I wouldn't give up my new independence for anything.'

'I wouldn't expect to be paid for helping a friend.'

Did this mean they were now friends? wondered Beth. Only a few minutes ago she'd believed he'd forget all about her as soon as their ways parted.

'That would be pushing the bounds of friendship a little too far, don't you think?'

'Is that what you think? In your opinion, how far could they be pushed?'

This was exactly the sort of conversation she wanted to avoid. It was straying too close to… *feelings*…for comfort. The combination of the wine and food, the warm evening, the soft glow of candlelight and the relaxed atmosphere Jensen had somehow managed to conjure from her stiff initial reception of his arrival had lulled her into dropping her guard. She thought about how she'd bumped into him earlier, in the doorway. His body had felt hard and yet not hostile against hers. If anything, those few seconds of contact between them had made her feel shielded and protected. It hadn't felt as if he'd wanted to pull away from her, as she had done from him.

What would have happened if she hadn't? If she'd been daring enough to take that minuscule step of not recoiling? If she'd put the palm of her hand flat on his muscled chest, just for a moment, would that still have been within the bounds of friendship, in his opinion, or would she have stepped over the boundary into hostile territory where she'd once thought she understood the rules, but found she didn't even speak the language?

A cold finger of apprehension touched her spine at the thought. Never, *never* again would she put herself in a position of giving her heart to someone, only for them to break it and throw it back at her. Jensen seemed to be honest, kind, dependable—all the qualities which she'd thought she'd found in Charles. She'd thought she'd *known* him. She'd never make such an assumption again, about anyone.

She'd thought she was a good judge of character, but her experience had proved her to be utterly wrong. She'd lost all faith in her own judgement. It had been proved to be completely flawed. Had she been so desperate for love and attention that she'd fallen for a man whose only consideration was the satisfaction of his own needs?

If so, she could never risk another relationship. She'd never be able to trust another man, but what was worse was that she didn't know when she'd ever be able to trust herself again, either.

On that last day, when Charles had run his fingers down her arm, circling her wrist, just tightly enough to be uncomfortable, it had suddenly made her skin crawl with a dread she hoped never to experience again. The words he'd spoken next had confirmed it.

'You must have misunderstood me, Beth. I've never given you any reason to believe this could be permanent...'

He'd let go of her wrist and she'd rubbed it, staring at him, but he'd turned away.

She wouldn't think about that. Not now. Not again.

'I...don't know. I hardly know you at all.'

'And yet, sitting here with you this evening, it feels as if I've known you for a long time,' he said, softly. 'How does it feel to you?'

Beth felt her heart thump and then pick up a faster rhythm. She pressed a hand to her side, trying to control it.

Her stomach swooped and she wished she hadn't had that extra glass of wine.

If feeling as if you could tell someone everything meant feeling you'd known them a long time, then yes, that was exactly how she felt. Trying to make sense of the emotions swirling through her was making her head spin, a little, and her hands shake. She had to wrest control back before she said or did something stupid.

Jensen was still, watchful, waiting for her answer and she knew he wouldn't let it go.

'No,' she said, knowing she was being untruthful. 'I feel as if I've known you for no time at all. But now I have a question for you.'

He raised his eyebrows a fraction and lifted his chin. 'You do?'

She hoped she could change the direction of the conversation. 'You don't usually sail alone. Why have you had this rather special bottle of wine in the locker above your berth for so long? Surely you must have had opportunities to drink it before now?'

CHAPTER EIGHT

JENSEN'S ATTENTION HAD been focussed on Beth's story, a slow-burning anger intensifying steadily at the way the behaviour of her possibly well-meaning but ultimately weak father had led to her being disinherited. If he had any spare mental or emotional space, he'd feel compelled to investigate the circumstances on her behalf.

But she'd made it clear that she had taken control of her own life, hinting that any interference wouldn't be welcome. He totally got that. She'd used her time here to confront her situation, choosing to make an attempt to shape a new life for herself. It couldn't have been easy, or comfortable, but she'd reached a point where she could at least consider looking for a new job.

From where he stood, that was great progress.

All this swirled in his mind while he studied her. She'd relaxed significantly as the evening wore on. She smiled more readily, and a lot of the tension seemed to have left her body. He didn't think the effects of the wine were solely responsible. When he'd first arrived and seen her, standing on the stairs, he'd been certain she'd been about to ask him to leave. Poised, wide-eyed, one hand on the banister, with her hair loose around her shoulders, she'd reminded him of something wild, on the point of flight.

But she hadn't fled. She'd faced up to whatever it was that was troubling her and come downstairs and she'd seemed to decide she could cope with him, as long as he didn't overstay his welcome.

He'd thought that she was vulnerable, behind her façade of competence, and he was right. But she'd faced up to her vulnerability, accepted what had happened, and decided to move on. Having the determination to do that gave her the strength of titanium.

He'd like to ask her how she'd done it, but he knew she wouldn't answer any more questions. She'd said making the garden had given her purpose and, no doubt, a focus. Well, he couldn't make a garden on *Sundance*, but he could focus on making his beloved yacht absolutely safe and shipshape again.

He'd been putting it off. Each time he'd tried to concentrate on a task, a maelstrom of negative thoughts had ambushed him and he'd given up. He wondered if Beth had experienced something similar. Had digging the hard, dry earth distracted her enough and worn her out sufficiently so that she was able to sleep, and to wake with a clear head and renewed purpose?

'Jensen?'

His attention snapped back to the present, and the problem. She'd turned the tables on him. Up until now, he'd been the one asking the questions. There was no reason why he shouldn't have bottles of wine on *Sundance*, but he'd let slip that this one had been there for a while.

'Ah, yes,' he said, taking his time, stretching his arms before clasping his hands behind his head. 'The wine.'

'What has kept you so busy over the past few years that you couldn't find an opportunity to share it with friends?'

He pushed his fingers into his temples, massaging the skin in small circles. 'Last summer, and the summer before that, I didn't sail at all. I was occupied with business affairs. It must have been, probably, two years before that when I bought half a dozen bottles of this in France. We were at Antibes for a few days and I took a trip into the winelands.'

'But you didn't drink everything you bought? I imagine storage space is at a premium on a yacht, especially for non-essential items, like bottles of wine.'

He smiled. 'That depends on your priorities, but you're right, there isn't a lot of space. Everything needs to be organised and tidy. This bottle was one that was overlooked.'

'And since then, you haven't been sailing with friends, or met any ashore? No one with whom you wanted to share it?'

Jensen shook his head. 'No. And I'm glad I didn't, because then I wouldn't have been able to share it with you.'

It hadn't been difficult to work out that she shied away from personal comments, compliments and questions. He hoped this would be enough to make her back off.

With mild satisfaction, but also a sharp twinge of regret, he saw that his strategy had worked. She straightened her knees, placing her feet under the table, and folded her hands in her lap.

'I've enjoyed the evening,' she said, formality creeping back into her voice, 'and thank you for choosing to share the wine with me.'

Jensen felt a little of his own tension release. 'At the end of that summer I left *Sundance* in a marina at Piraeus, in Greece. I picked her up again about five weeks ago.'

'Alone.'

'Yes, deliberately so. I needed a challenge. I hadn't sailed solo for a long time, and I'd begun to think that, at almost fifty, I was too old. Perhaps not fit enough. I wanted to prove I could still do it.' He sat forward, releasing his hands from behind his head and pressing his palms flat on the table. 'Now, let me help you tidy up and I'll be on my way.'

'Has it been hard?'

Her eyes were on his face and he didn't think he'd get away with anything less than the truth. And besides that, she deserved honesty.

'Sometimes, yes. Sometimes I thought I was going to have to admit defeat and give up. The need to be constantly on the lookout, the fatigue, wears you down and feels relentless at times. I tried to plan the trip so that I could be in a safe anchorage each night, but it wasn't always possible. There were nights when I could only snatch an hour, or less, of sleep at a time. But I kept going. It was important to me to do it. Crucial, actually. For a long time I'd known that I needed to get back to this place to think about things. Work things out. If I'd given up, I would have sacrificed a lot more than simply the journey.'

'Like what?' Her eyes were steady on his face, searching.

He huffed out a breath, suddenly aware that his breathing had become very shallow. How candid did he need to be? How much could he say without it being too much? His mind began to slide towards that familiar but dreaded downward spiral. He braced his hands on his thighs and breathed in, filling his lungs with the pure, sea-salted air.

'My self-belief,' he said, at last. His voice felt rough. 'Over time, there'd been circumstances that had tested it to the limit and I needed to re-establish it, rock-solid, in order to build…to rebuild…'

Jensen stopped. He was in danger of giving himself away. He tried to inhale deeply, again, past the knot that formed in his chest, when his stress levels mounted and his lungs felt squeezed. He stood, scraping his chair back on the tiles. He needed to leave.

He heard Beth follow him into the house as he carried their plates across to the kitchen. Would she question him further, or pick up on the fact that he didn't plan to say any more?

'Would you…?'

He turned towards her, still holding the plates, the cutlery piled on the top one in an untidy heap.

'I need to go…'

She stopped a few paces away from him. 'I was going to ask if you'd like a cup of coffee. A nightcap?'

The plates rattled as he placed them on the marble worktop. 'Oh…actually, no, thank you.' He pushed a hand through his hair, ruffling it. It hadn't been this long for thirty years. 'You must be tired after your long walk yesterday and gardening today. It's very warm.'

'I'm fine, thank you. And I'm grateful for your help yesterday.'

He smiled, relieved the questions had stopped. 'I was glad to help you. Thank you for an enjoyable evening.' He extended a hand towards her.

Whether it was because neither of them seemed in a hurry to break the contact between them this time, he wasn't sure, but somehow Beth was drawn towards him. He was conscious that her lips were slightly parted, her wide eyes pools of dark, shimmering green, and that he wanted to kiss her more than he'd wanted to kiss any woman for a very long time.

But he knew kissing her would be unforgivable of him. She'd given him no encouragement at all, and he'd be crossing a very strongly drawn boundary if he took that liberty. He'd ruin what could be a warm friendship, and for what? A few seconds of gratification taken at someone else's expense. That was not the sort of man he was.

He gave her hand a light squeeze and broke the contact.

'Goodnight.' Her voice was quiet.

'There was something else I meant to say.' He stepped back, towards the door. 'I've been thinking about what you said yesterday, and I think it'll help me to move on.'

Beth folded her arms, her head on one side. 'What did I say?'

He put his hand on the brass doorknob behind him. 'You said reaching the destination is only the beginning of the journey. For me, that's absolutely true, but if you hadn't said it, I don't think I would have realised it.'

* * *

Beth pushed the heavy door closed behind him and leaned her forehead against the cool wood. She wished she'd stepped up on her tiptoes and kissed him goodnight. His eyes, with that slight frown between them, had been on her mouth and she didn't think he'd have objected. But what if it hadn't been what he wanted?

Someone had tried to kiss her, once, against her will, and she remembered how angry she'd felt. It had been a drunken attempt by Steve, from Accounts, at the office Christmas party, who'd thought he'd caught her off guard under a bunch of mistletoe. She'd shoved him away before he'd even got close and the next day made it known that in future anyone behaving in a similar fashion would be reported to HR.

She thought the incident had cemented her in the role of ice maiden queen of the City.

Beth poured herself a glass of water and leaned against the kitchen island, tapping the glass against her lips.

What planet was she on? Perhaps the sun and spending all this time alone really had affected her ability to think logically and see straight. Romance was firmly off her agenda. She'd begun to get her life back under control and to at least see a way into the future. She did not need any complications. Definitely not a holiday fling. She packed the plates and glasses into the dishwasher and dropped the empty wine bottle into the bin.

The lesson that fairy tales did not come true had been a hard one, but she'd learned it well.

Jensen dragged the RIB across the beach, into the sea. He climbed in, not caring that his leather boat shoes were saturated with seawater. Then, instead of releasing the outboard motor down into the water, he pulled the oars from the bottom of the craft. He needed to expend some of his frustration in physical exercise. Manoeuvring the RIB so that the bow pointed towards the dim shape of *Sundance*, riding the slight swell in the middle of the cove, he put his back into the first stroke. The dinghy surged forwards with a satisfying leap, and he pulled again.

He'd been floored by the desire to kiss Beth. Her mouth had looked so soft and inviting, her eyes deep green pools, harbouring a question he couldn't interpret.

Could he have managed a friendly, goodnight peck on the cheek? No, he told himself, he couldn't. If his lips had so much as brushed her skin he'd have wanted it all, but she would not. He had nothing in the world to offer her, and he knew neither of them was the sort of person who would indulge in a holiday fling.

A woman like Beth—beautiful, intelligent and with new-found freedom and independence—

could have her pick of men, when she chose to. And if she ever discovered his true circumstances, the reason he was hiding from the world in a remote cove in Turkey, she'd want to put the width of the Mediterranean between them.

She'd get another job, with someone who appreciated her dedication and loyalty, and, with the right advice, he thought she could successfully claim something from her stepmother's estate.

Whereas he... There was no certainty, at all, that he'd ever recover. There was no way back to his old life and he hadn't yet figured out a way forward into a life where everything had changed.

She'd said the journey could only begin, now he'd reached his destination. He had to hang onto that belief and find the start of his new path. He just wasn't sure he believed it existed yet.

So what the hell was he doing, even thinking about kissing Beth? He'd sworn off women. They'd all proved shallow and disloyal, deleting him from their lives as soon as things had gone wrong.

There was no reason, at all, why Beth would be any different.

Glancing over his shoulder, Jensen altered his course slightly and nudged the RIB up to the platform at *Sundance*'s stern, leaping aboard and securing the mooring. He climbed up the short ladder to the cockpit and then onto the deck. He waited for the familiar feeling of safety and comfort to envelop him, but this evening it was absent, adding fuel to the frustration that simmered through his veins. The trip across the water to *Sundance* had not been nearly long enough. It would take a couple of miles of hard rowing, at least, for the exertion to have a therapeutic effect on his mind or exhaust his body enough to enable him to crash out on the deck and sleep.

It was a relief to ease his feet out of his wet shoes and strip off his jeans and shirt, welcoming the slight, cooling breeze that hummed softly in the rigging and whispered across his heated skin. He stared back at the shoreline, where the trees were a darker, more dense mass than the surrounding headlands and sky, but tonight, as every other night, there was no glimpse of a light from the villa that he knew was there, sheltering a woman who, rightly or wrongly, was someone he thought, in spite of all his angry protestations, he wanted in his flawed life.

There was an odd sort of relief in admitting that. Stretching out on his unrolled mat and pulling a cotton sheet over himself, gazing up at the dark sky and dewy stars, he tried to get his thoughts into some sort of logical order.

He wanted her in his life, in whatever form possible. But the words that flashed, in neon-bright colours, in his brain were: You can't have her.

CHAPTER NINE

TWO LONG DAYS LATER, Beth was buzzing with un-
expended energy. Her routine of swimming in the
morning and evening had been wrecked by the
injury to her heel. Gardening was limited by the
heat. The mornings and afternoons had merged
into one, time dragging in the stillness.

It was tempting to blame Jensen for her unset-
tled spirit. She'd been happy in the rhythm she'd
established before he'd arrived, but she knew she
had allowed his presence to disturb her more than
she should have done. She wondered if he was
all right. Did he need help but was too proud to
ask for it?

She should have been pleased that he appeared
to be staying away from her. It was what they'd
both said they wanted, after all.

Why, then, did her eyes keep returning to the
gap in the trees where the path from the beach
emerged? Was she subconsciously willing him
to appear?

As the shadows lengthened towards the second

evening, she poured herself a glass of pomegranate juice and carried it out onto the terrace, risking the heat even though she knew she couldn't cool off in the pool. But she'd removed the dressing from her foot and from tomorrow nothing would keep her out of the water.

Early the following morning, listening intently, she could not hear the telltale tapping of *Sundance*'s rigging, but there was not even the trace of a breeze, so that wasn't a guarantee that the boat had gone. But perhaps he had left, leaving her well behind him. She sipped her morning coffee, and knew she had to find out.

She'd dressed in her bikini, in anticipation of her first swim for several days, and she pulled her kaftan over it, picked up her sunglasses and slipped her feet into her flip-flops.

The cove was at its peaceful best. Glassy ripples pushed onto the beach, lit by the low sun, and the rocks cast long, dense shadows onto the limpid water.

Sundance lay at her anchor, like a vision from another age, her graceful lines immaculate. The scene was so perfect that Beth caught her breath. She slid her feet out of her flip-flops onto the sand, which was still cool under her feet, and pulled the kaftan over her head, leaving it with her sunglasses at the edge of the trees. Then she walked down to the water's edge and waded in.

This was the time they'd agreed she would use the beach, and from today she intended to claim it. A new confidence and energy lightened her step. Jensen was free to leave, if he didn't like her presence on the beach, or if he needed anything he could seek her out.

The silky water was just cool enough to raise goosebumps across her skin. She stood, ripples lapping around her thighs, and then took a deep breath and dived in, surfaced and struck out in a steady front crawl across the cove.

When she reached the overhanging rocks around the rim of the bay, she stopped and rolled onto her back, floating. The morning sky had lost the rosy tinge of dawn and was deepening to its summer azure. Golden sunlight lit the crest of each ripple around her. The only sounds were those of the sea, the only movement the water.

She rolled over, relishing being back in the sea, and began swimming towards the beach in a measured breaststroke. A slight splash behind her made her turn her head, and Jensen emerged from the water, flicking his hair from his eyes.

'Hey.'

His voice carried clearly across the water and she raised a hand to acknowledge his greeting, finding she was back within her depth, the shingle tickling the soles of her feet. Jensen swam towards her, his powerful arms cutting through the water with barely a splash.

Beth waded onto the beach. She wanted to carry on walking until she reached her kaftan and sunglasses, both of which would provide cover, but she knew he'd reach her first. And anyway, she decided, she was over trying to hide herself away. Recognising the uncertainty he'd allowed her to see in him had added a layer to her own confidence. She squared her shoulders, turned, waiting for him.

He pushed his hair back and wiped a hand over his face.

'Hi.' She folded her arms. 'Your leg looks better.'

'It is, thank you. I'll return what's left of the comfrey. It worked wonders on the bruising.' He looked down at her feet. 'Your blister must have healed.'

'I'm celebrating with a swim in the sea.'

'According to our plan. I apologise for being here. I no longer expected you to come down to the beach. But I'm glad you have.'

'How are the repairs to *Sundance* coming on?'

His smile was a little crooked. 'Do you mean when might I be leaving?'

'That's not what I meant at all, although in this still weather I can't hear the tapping of the rigging so I don't know if you're here or not.'

'I've finally managed to settle down and get on with the list of things that need doing. The repairs are going well, now. The past two days have been pretty busy. I need to take her out for some gentle sea trials.'

Beth looked beyond him, to where *Sundance* drifted serenely on her anchor. She wondered if she was as beautiful below decks as she was above. Was there a neat galley and a cosy saloon, or was it stripped back and spartan?

'If you take her for a sail, could I come with you?' The words were out of her mouth before she'd even thought them. She felt shocked at herself. 'But you won't need a novice on board when you're testing things out. I might be...' She stopped in mid-sentence. Jensen was regarding her with such surprise that it made her smile. 'What?'

'Nothing.' He shook his head, looking bemused. 'That is... I wasn't expecting that. But I... I'd love to take you sailing. Have you ever sailed before?' The corners of his mouth lifted and her stomach turned over. It was such a gentle smile. 'Is there any particular reason why?'

'Just...for fun? And I imagine it's cooler out on the water.'

'It is. And it would be fun.'

'I must warn you that I don't know how to sail. When I was little my father used to take me to the Round Pond in Kensington Gardens to watch the model boats. I thought it looked difficult.'

He laughed, his hands on his hips. 'You don't have to be able to sail to come out with me. Not even a model boat. It's not difficult. I'll do the work. All you'll have to do is enjoy yourself.'

'I might be sick. Or afraid. The only boat I've ever been on is a cross-channel ferry from Dover to Calais and I was ill.'

'If you feel queasy, I can give you a motion sickness tablet, and there is no need to be afraid. I've been sailing for most of my life, and I haven't lost a man overboard in…let me see…ever. If you really want to come, I hope very much that you might enjoy it.'

She gripped her hands together and raised her eyes to look beyond him, out towards the sea.

'Where would we go?'

'We'll go out between the headlands and, if the wind is favourable, turn south-west.'

'And if it's not?'

'If it's not, we'll turn north-east, but the south-west will be more interesting.'

'Oh…why is that?'

'You'll see when we get there. When would you like to go?'

'When could you?' Beth felt a mixture of excitement and apprehension dance in her stomach. She could hardly believe she'd instigated this, but the idea had taken hold now and she knew she wouldn't back out. It would be a new experience, to push her out of her comfort zone and test her resilience.

'There're a couple of things I still need to check,

but by tomorrow morning she'll be ready to go.' He turned and began to wade back into the sea. 'I'll pick you up in the RIB on the beach at around eight if that's not too early for you.' He spoke over his shoulder. 'Bring a hat and sunscreen, and a tee shirt in case you want to cover up,' he called, before diving into the water.

She'd half hoped he might say today. But was the idea of having to cling to a tilting deck while being splashed with seawater and probably feeling sick a good one? On the other hand, if it meant spending the day with a handsome man in whose company she felt comfortable, and who seemed to enjoy hers, it couldn't be a bad one.

It was just before eight o'clock when Jensen steered the RIB through the calm early morning sea. He scanned the beach, but he couldn't see any sign of Beth. The bottom of the dinghy scraped on the shingle and he jumped out, holding onto the mooring rope.

The sun was up but the morning shadows were long and the air still held a breath of freshness. The heat would ramp up during the day, but out on the water they'd be kept cool by the sea breezes. He was looking forward to feeling *Sundance* come alive beneath his feet and hands again, and to the sensation of freedom, which setting sail always brought to him. He hoped, very much, that Beth would feel a bit of it, too.

A movement caught his eye and he saw her emerge from the line of trees behind the beach. He blew out a long breath, finally allowing himself to admit that he'd been afraid she might not show up.

She was wearing the embroidered cotton kaftan that reached to mid-thigh and her hair was pulled into a ponytail, which swung as she walked. It was a compromise between the severe, pinned-up style she usually favoured, and the loose-around-the-shoulders relaxed look that he thought was beautiful. A cloth bag hung from her shoulder.

'You came. Good morning.'

'Did you think I might not?' Her gaze met his, holding a faint challenge.

'I would have come looking for you, if you hadn't.'

Ripples of water curled onto the shingle, but as they'd washed in they'd lifted the RIB and it had bobbed a little further out and it was now floating, a few yards away. Jensen tugged on the rope to bring it closer in. He held out a hand.

'Pass me your bag.'

He waded through the water and deposited the bag in the boat. Then he held the RIB steady with one hand. Beth was beside him, stepping into the boat. She wobbled and put a hand on his shoulder, steadying herself, and then she sat down on the wooden plank, which formed the seat.

'Okay?' He had to work at keeping his voice

neutral. The rosemary and lavender scent of her hair had swamped his senses, and the soft touch of her hand on his shoulder felt like a caress.

She nodded. 'Yes. Thank you.' She pulled her bag towards her and took out a pair of sunglasses, putting them on. 'I'll need these.'

Jensen climbed in, taking care not to splash her, and started the outboard motor. As he turned the boat and set a course towards *Sundance*, Beth's hands came down by the sides of her hips and her fingers curled around the edge of the plank, but her back remained straight. This might have been her idea, but he could see she was out of her comfort zone. The fact that she'd deliberately put herself there sent his admiration of her climbing several notches.

He hopped onto the platform at *Sundance*'s stern, secured the tow rope and held out a hand to Beth. Lip caught between her teeth, she straightened her knees and stood, wobbly and unsure, and clung to his fingers. As she negotiated the transfer from the dinghy to *Sundance* she swayed and he caught her, holding her encircled in one arm.

'You're okay.' That perfume assaulted his senses again. 'Up that little ladder and you'll be in the cockpit, where it all happens.'

He would not let her see how her nearness affected him. She'd put herself in his care, doing something new and, no doubt, scary, and he'd never, ever take advantage of that. She looked unsure and conflicted, but she hadn't backed out of the trip. She had courage and determination, which he would do his best to emulate.

Beth climbed the few rungs of the ladder and swung herself into the cockpit. She sat down hurriedly. Even at anchor, the gentle sway of *Sundance* beneath her feet was disconcerting. It suddenly felt as if all her usual points of reference had been altered or removed. She felt untethered, and very vulnerable. She was, she admitted to herself, on a boat with a man whom she hardly knew, and completely dependent on him for her safe return to dry land and the villa.

Nobody else in the world knew where she was.

Although the thought might have been alarming, it was also oddly liberating. She felt empowered by her decision to try out something completely new and different. It was an opportunity that might never present itself again and she needed to savour it, even if in the end she didn't enjoy it.

Jensen had joined her in the cockpit.

'Now you're wondering what you've done.' He sat down on the bench a few feet away. 'Alone at sea with a strange man.'

She nodded. 'Exactly. Somehow, I've allowed this to happen.'

'By the end of the day you won't want to go

home.' He flashed a smile at her. 'Let me show you *Sundance*.'

Beth could feel that Jensen was in his element. He moved with ease around the complicated cockpit, his footing sure, his big hands familiar with all the strange pieces of equipment that mystified her.

She followed him up two steps onto the varnished deck. He led her towards the bow and pointed to where cushions were arranged against the side of the projecting roof above the space below the decks.

'Make yourself comfortable here.' He dropped her bag onto the deck. 'You'll be able to see where we're going. We'll be motoring out between the headlands, but you'll be out of the way of the boom once I put the sail up.'

'Where *are* we going?' Beth dropped to her knees before settling herself, cross-legged, on the cushions. 'Have you decided?'

'It's a perfect wind for sailing down the coast. Have you heard of Kekova Island?'

'No.' Beth shook her head and adjusted her sunglasses.

'We'll head that way. It's a small, uninhabited island where the ancient city of Dolichiste once stood, until an earthquake, one morning in the second century, sent it sliding into the sea.' He propped one hand against the foremast. 'Now most of the ruins are underwater, although some can still be seen on the shoreline and the rocky slopes above.'

'It sounds a bit creepy.'

'On a storm-tossed winter's night, it might be, but in the sunshine on a day like today it's interesting. Shall we go and take a look?'

Beth heard the quiet hum of *Sundance*'s engine starting up and watched as the anchor chain hauled the anchor from the seabed. As the yacht passed between the two headlands that sheltered the cove, almost hiding it from the open sea, she wondered how Jensen had navigated his way through this narrow passage, in the dark, on a damaged boat. The knowledge that he must be a skilful sailor gave her confidence a boost.

The creaking in the rigging and snapping of the mainsail as it unfurled from the boom and rose up the mast was unnerving, but then the big sail filled with the breeze, the sound of the engine died, and *Sundance* was rising and dipping gently, a creamy wave curling away from the bow as she cleaved through the aquamarine water.

It wasn't anything like Beth had expected. It was serene and beautiful.

Jensen appeared at her side and she glanced towards the stern, a little wave of anxiety pulsing through her.

'Shouldn't you be steering, or something?' She remembered the big, spoked wheel in the cockpit.

'Don't look so worried, Beth. There's a self-steering rig, but I won't leave the wheel for long. I'm only going to raise one sail today. It'll be less lively that way.'

He disappeared towards the stern and Beth relaxed in the cushions, determined to enjoy the experience and the view of the coast, with its inlets and coves, rocky slopes and scrubby hills. The slap of the water against the hull and the occasional hiss of a small wave cresting and breaking was rhythmic and soothing. She settled herself more comfortably and propped a cushion behind her head, against the mast.

If this was sailing, she could definitely get to like it.

She woke with a start, remembering where she was and sitting bolt upright. It was quiet. *Sundance* was barely moving through the water and the sail had been furled.

Jensen crouched in front of her, his face creased in a smile. He'd taken off his tee shirt.

'Good sleep? You must have been tired.'

Beth rubbed a hand over her face, trying to pretend she hadn't noticed his broad shoulders and the sprinkling of dark hair, mixed with silver, over his chest. 'I didn't sleep too well last night.' That was an understatement. She'd hardly slept at all, nervous anticipation stalking her waking moments and her restless sleep. 'But it was so peaceful, and the sounds of the water were soothing. I didn't mean to drop off, but…'

'That's Kekova Island, on the starboard side. We'll motor closer in and you'll be able to see the ruins, if you like.'

Beth nodded. She glanced up at the sun, now high in the deep blue sky. 'I'd better put on some sunscreen.'

'Would you like me to do your back?'

'I'm not going to take my kaftan off…' too late, she saw the teasing lift of the corner of his mouth '…since I'm not planning to go swimming,' she finished. 'But I could do yours.'

'We can't go swimming. Swimming and diving have been forbidden here. Too many visitors were taking artefacts home as souvenirs. And yes, thank you, you could.'

'Have we anchored?' She pulled her bag towards her. 'I'll find my sunscreen.'

'No, we're drifting, for a minute.' He stood up. 'Come astern to the cockpit. There's sunscreen in the locker. You can do my back while I find us somewhere to anchor for lunch.'

She followed Jensen back along the deck, down into the cockpit, where his tee shirt lay on the bench seating. With one hand resting on the wheel, he reached into a locker and pulled out a tube of sunscreen, handing it to her. He replaced his hand on the wheel and stood with his back to her, bronzed bare feet planted on the deck, his powerful thighs braced apart.

Beth looked out at the quiet island as the coast slipped past them. It was more beautiful than she'd ever expected. Somehow, getting here on Jensen's yacht made the whole experience more empowering and satisfying; so much better than being on a tourist boat, with a loud commentary in several different languages. It was exhilarating to stand on the gently moving deck, her hand on the rail, and watch the scenery slide by. At that moment, she didn't think she'd have changed places with anyone in the world.

Was she really the same Beth who'd arrived in Turkey, her spirit crushed, her confidence at rock bottom, and fear of the future overshadowing every moment?

That version of her would have been horrified at the idea of putting sunscreen onto Jensen's back. She'd never put sunscreen on anyone but herself, and the thought of running her hands over his muscled shoulders would have been terrifying.

But none of those emotions troubled her now. How hard could it be, to squeeze cream from a tube and spread it onto skin? She smiled at the realisation of how far behind she'd left her previous self, acknowledging, at the same time, that her interaction with Jensen had helped her. He'd demonstrated kind consideration towards her, and talking to him about her family relationships had been therapeutic. Afterwards, she'd realised with surprise that she'd never discussed them with anyone else at all.

She stood still, holding the tube in one hand, and let go of the railing with the other.

'Beth?' Jensen glanced over his shoulder. 'Are you okay?' There was a gentle note of intimate teasing in his voice, as if he thought she might be wishing she hadn't volunteered for this task.

'I'm fine. Just loving the view.' Two could tease. She flipped up the lid and squeezed some of the cream from the tube into the palm of her hand, and launched herself into another new experience.

His skin shivered as she dabbed the cream across his shoulders. 'That's cold.'

'Your skin is so warm.' With care, she smoothed the palms of her hands over his tanned skin, feeling the muscles bunch and flex beneath her touch. 'That's why it feels cold.'

'It's also good. Thank you.'

The flat blades of his shoulders pulled down alongside his spine as his upper back moved in. She rubbed the cream into his skin, her confidence growing. His chin dipped towards his chest as her fingers massaged the base of his neck and then fanned out, moving down over his ribs, her thumbs circling each individual vertebra. She added more cream, wondering at how simple and curiously natural it felt to be standing behind a man, on a yacht, massaging cream into his back.

Suddenly, Jensen's head went up and he stepped sideways, away from her.

'Thank you. That feels great.'

'I haven't quite finished. There's still some left to rub in.'

'I need to drop the anchor,' he said, an edge of urgency sharpening his voice. 'We're getting too close to the rocks.' He left the cockpit and strode along the deck, out of her sight.

Beth pressed the cap back onto the sunscreen and replaced it in the locker. If he hadn't said how good it was she'd have thought he hadn't liked it.

Jensen gripped the railing at *Sundance*'s bow and leaned forwards. He ducked his head and took several deep breaths of the salt-laden air, trying to exert some degree of control over the off-the-scale reaction of his body.

There was a straightforward explanation, he told himself. He hadn't felt a woman's touch for so long that naturally he—*his body*—was bound to overreact. But when, he wondered, had he ever felt anything more sensual than the gentle, firm, caressing strokes across his back that Beth had administered?

Had she genuinely no idea of the effect it had been having on him? Was that what had made it so erotic? He'd had to clench his jaw, straighten his spine, try to move away to lessen the pressure of her fingers on the most sensitive places on his back. But her hands seemed to know where every single pleasure zone was, and nothing he'd done had stopped the electrifying, white-hot darts of sensation that had arrowed straight down to his lower abdomen, creating all kinds of havoc.

Where had the anxious, defensive woman he'd met on the beach that first morning gone? She seemed to have vanished without trace, to be replaced by this new version. She even looked different. Some of her hair blew around her face, having escaped the ponytail she wore it in today. Her tense expression had softened into one of enjoyment and happiness. But most of all she exuded a new sense of quiet self-confidence and positivity.

Had he changed, too? He remembered how angry he'd felt when he'd discovered that a house had been built above *his* secret cove; that a woman was living in it, who claimed the beach and cove as her own. He'd felt cheated; as if his long, sometimes dangerous voyage had been in vain; as if the world, which had already dealt him the worst possible hand, were laughing at him for thinking he might still defeat the odds.

He hadn't been able to escape defeat. When he'd stopped moving, instead of finding solace, he'd been overcome with negativity and destructive thoughts, revenge uppermost in his mind.

But those had faded. Perhaps the place had exerted its magic, after all, with a subtlety he'd been unaware of. But perhaps, with her acceptance of him at face value, Beth had shown that only a small part of the world despised him. Not everyone needed him only for what he could give them, and when that had turned to nothing, they'd all deserted him.

Beth had told him that his journey was only just beginning, without knowing the impossible path he was on, but he'd realised she was right. He'd had to stop running and allow everything he was running from to catch up with him. Then, when he'd examined his demons, he'd found they didn't stand up to detailed scrutiny, after all. They were mostly in his head. Rather than trying to block them from his mind, he had to admit them, and then let them go, without attaching any value to them.

That was how to rob them of their power.

Over the past few days he'd found a measure of peace, and the space that had created in his head was allowing him to appreciate this day, in the moment. Beth wanted nothing from him at all, and in return he found he wanted to give her everything.

He'd wanted to abandon the wheel, turn and take her in his arms but that was beyond impossible. He thought she was beginning to trust him, otherwise she'd never have put herself in this vulnerable position, alone with him. She'd feel threatened and trapped if he touched her. He would do anything to nurture that trust.

Sundance had, he noticed with a shock, now really drifted too close to the rocky shore for safety. Trying to gather up the shreds of his self-control, he forced himself back into action. Not only had he allowed his body to almost overrule his mind, but the consequences of his lack of control had put them in a position of possible danger.

He'd told Beth he was a competent, safe sailor. Landing them on the rocks was not going to happen. He released the anchor, hoping it would secure them at the first try, and then returned to the cockpit.

'Jensen?' He heard her call before he saw her. She was standing before the wheel, peering forward to see where he was.

'Yeah. I'm here.' He leapt down into the cockpit, took the wheel and motored forward, over where the anchor should be, before cutting the engine and allowing *Sundance* to drift astern until the chain pulled taut.

'Are you okay? Did I do something wrong?'

From somewhere he conjured up a smile. 'Of course not. What could you have done wrong?'

She'd done everything right.

'You just seem a bit…distracted. Is this where we're having lunch?'

Distracted was one way of putting it. Body on

fire, brain turned to sponge, heartbeat out of control was another.

'It is. I'll go below and get some food. It's very simple.'

He disappeared down the companionway into *Sundance*'s spacious galley.

'Do you need help?' Beth's face appeared in the hatch above him. 'Can I come down?'

'Turn around and come down backwards, at least the first time. It's steep.'

He stepped back as Beth's feet appeared, her right heel still red where the blister had healed. Now he wondered how he'd managed to apply that dressing without self-combusting. Her long, shapely legs followed, her skin a pale, polished gold. He pushed his hands into his pockets to prevent them from reaching out and resting on her waist, to help her down the last two steps.

'It's so beautiful. And so tidy!' She looked round, wide-eyed. 'I had no idea it would be so… luxurious. Will you give me a tour?'

Jensen followed her through the dining area to the adjoining salon with its panelled walls and dark green leather seating.

'There're two cabins through those doors, and a bathroom.' He thought she might have seen enough, but she pushed the door open and carried on. 'The master cabin and bathroom are in the forward section.'

'It's amazing. I love it. Everything has a place.'

She ran a hand over the gleaming wood, her eyes shining.

'It's really important to keep things tidy below decks. And everything has to have a secure place so that nothing goes flying in rough weather.'

Beth bent to look through a porthole. 'That's hard to imagine, on a day like today. I wouldn't like rough conditions.'

'You might surprise yourself. To pitch yourself and your craft against the wind and the sea is exhilarating.'

She'd reached the master cabin. 'This looks super comfortable.'

The wide berth was made up in fine cotton bedlinen, with deep pillows and a knobbly cotton throw folded across the foot. The glimpse into the en suite bathroom showed gleaming chrome, tiles and porcelain.

Jensen stood at the door. 'I suppose it does.'

'Is this where you sleep?'

He shrugged, putting a hand up onto the doorframe above his head. 'No.' He shook his head. 'I...sleep on the deck. I prefer to be in the open.'

He hoped she was too star-struck by the cabin to probe him for reasons. He also wanted to get her away from that soft, wide bed, before his wayward brain began to imagine uses for it that did not involve sleeping, and his body, just recently talked into submission, called in reinforcements and rebelled again, testing his determination to the limit.

Beth walked past him, back towards the galley, her hips swaying beneath her loose kaftan and her ponytail swinging as she moved. Jensen rubbed a hand over the back of his neck before following her, wishing he could stop acting and reacting like the teenager he'd been over thirty years ago.

'This is all so tasty. Thank you.' Beth wiped the last piece of flatbread around the bowl of hummus and popped it into her mouth before reaching for a piece of rose-scented Turkish delight from a small tin. Powdered sugar clung to her lips as she bit into it, finding the soft sweetness studded with crunchy pistachio nuts. 'Those olives are the nicest I've ever tasted, and this is the perfect dessert.'

She'd let Jensen persuade her to have a glass of wine and she felt deliciously relaxed. Eating al fresco on board a yacht was a brand-new experience and possibly about to become her favourite pastime. She pulled up her knees and leaned against the bulkhead, watching Jensen stack the bowls and plates.

'Ready to look at the ruins?' He disappeared, carrying the remains of their lunch down into the galley before reappearing and getting ready to get under way again. Beth joined him in the cockpit, leaning over the side.

In the depths of the crystal-clear water, the ruins of the ancient city, which had slipped down the mountainside almost two thousand years ago, floated into ghostly view. The steps of a staircase, carved from stone, curved down into the water and disappeared in the shadows far below. The foundations of a house were clearly visible, and what had been a harbour wall jutted out from the shore.

'It's extraordinary,' she said, her voice low. 'All this, destroyed in a few moments of volcanic upheaval. There were people living here, going about their lives, when suddenly everything changed for ever...' He saw her brows draw together in a frown. 'It really brings home that thing about second chances.'

'What thing?'

'You know, how we all believe we'll have a second chance at something if we mess up the first time around. There'll always be a tomorrow to improve on today. But for all these people—' she trailed her fingers in the water '—it never came.'

Above the waterline were the ruins of houses, water channels and pipes.

'Dolichiste was an important trading hub in the ancient Mediterranean,' Jensen said, slowing *Sundance*'s engine to an idle throb. 'Its catastrophic destruction must have had far-reaching effects.'

'It's like a living museum. I'm glad swimming

and diving have been prohibited. Even looking down at the ruins from here feels almost intrusive.' Beth straightened up. 'Thank you for bringing me. It's something I'll never forget.'

Jensen squinted up at the sun. 'Not quite over the yardarm, but I think we should make our way back. The wind is freshening and we'll be sailing into it. It'll be a longer journey.'

Beth looked out across the water. It was calm in the lee of the shore, but a little choppy. White waves danced out in the main channel. Anxiety lurched in her stomach.

'Oh. Will it be rough?'

'Not rough. Just more brisk than it was this morning. If you don't like it, you can go below and make yourself comfortable in the salon or on one of the berths. The wind will be stronger up on deck this afternoon. We'll be sailing on a close-hauled reach and then coming about and motoring back through the headlands under the power of the engine.'

'Most of that sounds like a foreign language to me, but I think I'd prefer to stay up here with you. I like to know what's happening.'

'That's good. I'd like you to stay up with me.'

The wind held steady as Jensen set a course that would bring them opposite the entrance to their cove. With the sail pulled in tight he aimed to sail as close to the wind as he could. *Sundance* responded swiftly to the adjustments he made and she heeled away from the wind, picking up speed, her starboard beam close to the water.

Jensen pulled a towel out of a locker and tossed it to Beth. 'Wrap yourself up in this. There'll be some spray coming into the cockpit.' He glanced at her face. She was chalk-white and gripping the edge of the seat with both hands. 'Are you feeling ill?'

Beth shook her head. 'Not ill. Just…scared.' She ducked as a sheet of spray arched over them.

'There's no need to be afraid, but I understand it's scary if this is your first time on the water.' He braced his legs against the kick of the deck as *Sundance* slapped back onto the surface after cresting a slightly larger swell. 'Move up this way.' He nodded to a corner of the cockpit. 'It'll be more sheltered.'

Beth released the death grip she appeared to have on the seat and shuffled along, pulling the towel over her shoulders and drawing her knees up underneath it. He reached out with one hand and tucked the edges of the towel around her neck, briefly cupping her cheek in his palm. He hoped the gesture might reassure her. 'I'll get us home as quickly and as comfortably as I can,' he called. 'If you can relax you might enjoy the ride.'

He hoped she would. He'd watched her unfurl today, opening as a flower opened its petals to the warmth and light of the sun, and watching it happen was addictive. He wanted more. He wanted her to love this day, to remember it as one of the best days of her life and to feel the excitement he felt as *Sundance* skimmed over the water. He didn't want it spoilt by her anxiety or fear.

He kept the yacht on a steady course, not allowing her to heel over too much. It was a beautiful, breezy, sun-filled afternoon, the best kind of day for sailing, and they were making excellent headway. For the first time in many months, a sense of exhilaration and freedom took hold of him. It was more—far more—than physical freedom. It felt, at last, like freedom of the soul.

Another burst of spray fanned out over the cockpit and he heard Beth gasp. Expecting to see her cowering beneath the towel, he was surprised to find she'd let it slip around her shoulders and that her face was lit by a smile.

'The spray was filled with rainbow colours,' she exclaimed. 'We were under our own rainbow. It's magical.'

A rush of relief made him laugh out loud. Beth had begun to enjoy herself again. 'Not so bad?'

'I think it's not so bad at all. In fact, it's very, very good.'

He laughed again, throwing his head back, feeling his over-long hair blowing in the wind and noticing that Beth's ponytail had come undone and her hair was dancing around her shoulders. She was learning to trust him, and it was the best feeling in the world.

'Once we get into the lee of the hills, closer to the shore, it'll be calmer.' He looked over his shoulder, and when he turned back he was surprised to find Beth standing up, keeping herself steady with one hand on the rail.

'Jensen?'

He leaned towards her, concerned. 'Are you okay?'

'Will you show me how to steer *Sundance*? Just for a minute. I really want to see how it feels.'

'Of course.' A rush of feeling, a mixture of relief and joy, washed over him. He wanted to share this unique, exquisite sensation of living in the moment, for the moment, with her, and he loved that she wanted it, too.

'Are you sure it'll be safe?'

'I won't let anything bad happen to you, Beth. Trust me.'

It felt odd, suggesting she should trust him. Trust was a luxury that had been taken away from him the moment he'd been accused of the theft of funds from the charity of which he was the CEO. The sense of disbelief that such an accusation could be levelled at him still took his breath away when he remembered that chaotic day. He'd been suspended, barred from the office, left with nothing to do but protest his innocence. Even then, he'd believed it would all be okay. A mistake would be found. An apology made. Everything would return to normal.

Nothing would ever be normal again. As soon as the shadow of suspicion had fallen on him, he'd been viewed with distrust. His friends, colleagues and, worst of all, his family, had distanced themselves from him, as if they themselves might be tainted by association with him. The court case had been a nightmare, which still revisited him frequently in his sleep. The aggression of the prosecution had floored him, and the verdict bewildered him.

The determination of the one friend who'd kept faith in him had kept him from sinking into the depths of depression. James had rallied support, mounted his own investigation, never given up, and Jensen had been proved innocent, after all.

Perhaps other friends would be willing to bury the past now, but would he still want them as friends? No, he would not. The only person with whom he wanted, desperately, to engage was his fifteen-year-old daughter. The knowledge that Emily had refused to speak to him ever since he'd been accused was too painful to confront or accept. What if she never changed her mind? The thought felt like something sharp, which twisted in his chest and almost made him gasp for air. Anyone else could go to hell, but Emily… He was, he admitted, too afraid to try to make contact with her, in case she rebuffed him. He didn't know if he could bear that.

Beth knew none of that. If she trusted him, it was without prejudice, on the basis of what she'd learned about him in a few days. This time they were spending together would be perfect and unspoiled by any of his history.

He guided *Sundance* into calmer waters as the twin headlands appeared on the port bow. Their speed dropped a little, and he hauled in the sail more tightly. Then he put out a hand to Beth.

She took it, wobbling a little, the towel dropping to her feet. He pulled her towards him, making space for her between his body and the wheel.

'Put your hands here, and here,' he said from behind her, and then placed his hands over hers. 'Hold on like this, not too tightly, and get the feel of the boat. Don't fight it. Control it, but with as light a touch as possible.'

Her shoulders and arms were rigid, her jaw tense.

'It feels as though it's fighting me, not the other way round.'

'Try to relax your shoulders and arms, or tomorrow you'll feel as if you've done a weights session at the gym.'

'I've never lifted weights, so I won't recognise that feeling.'

He was pleased she felt relaxed enough to joke, and he saw her making an effort to release the tension in her muscles. Her hands softened a little under his, and she flexed her fingers.

'That's better. Much better. Do you see that headland beyond us? Try to keep the bow lined up with that. That course will bring us to the right place.'

Sundance's bow plunged into an unexpected trough and Beth swayed on her feet, clutching at the wheel and pulling her slightly off course.

'Sorry. That was wrong, wasn't it?'

'That was fine, Beth. Don't beat yourself up. Nobody gets it right the first time. You can't predict or fight the sea. You just have to learn to go with it.' He moved closer to her, so that if it happened again she'd feel safe from falling. His arms closed round her shoulders and her back pressed against his chest. 'You're doing really well.' He bent his head to speak into her ear and she half turned towards him. His mouth brushed against her cheek.

He expected her to pull away, or flinch, but instead she tilted her head to look at him.

'I'm not sure I can steer with you so close. It does funny things to my sense of direction.'

'Just keep your hands on the wheel. I'll steer for both of us, if you want me to?' He waited for her nod of assent and then lifted his right hand and wrapped his arm around her waist, pulling her gently against him and holding her there.

'I think I do,' she murmured. 'As long as you

keep holding me like that, and don't ask me if we're going north or south.'

'I would like to.' His voice felt impeded. 'But I'm going to have to drop the sail and start the engine.' He tightened his hold on her for a moment, then took the wheel in both hands again, turning *Sundance* into the wind. She slowed almost to a stop, her sail flapping above them. 'Hold her there, Beth, and I'll be right back.'

When he returned, putting his arms around her again felt like coming back to a safe place. The sail was safely furled and he pressed the ignition button, feeling the vibration of the engine starting up below the deck.

'I won't be able to steer through the headlands, Jensen. You'll have to do it.' Her voice trembled slightly.

'It's okay, I'll help you. Just stay where you are.' He rested his chin on the top of her head, for a brief second. She stepped back a little and he felt her curves pressing into his thighs. His breath jammed in his throat. 'Beth...'

'Mmm?'

'That's...almost too much.'

He felt lit up and properly alive for the first time in a year. She wanted to be with him, not because of who he had been, but simply because she enjoyed his company. The fact that she might make him buzz with need and, yes, desire, did not seem to occur to her.

* * *

The experiences of the day had been liberating for Beth. She couldn't remember another time—apart from her final day at work, and she'd rather forget that—when she'd deliberately done something outside her comfort zone, and the buzz it had given her had been incredible. Over the course of a few months, she'd lost her home and her job, and with it her self-belief. She'd been left with no anchor, no safe space, until she'd made a temporary one in the villa in Turkey.

But today she'd discovered she no longer needed to be bound by those insecurities. She'd dared to let herself go and found she hadn't been sucked into a frightening, unknown vacuum. She'd met challenges and enjoyed them. She felt ready to meet more.

Jensen made her feel safe. Infinitely safe. It was a deeper level of emotion than anything she'd ever experienced. It should have been frightening, but it simply felt exciting, something she was eager to explore further. He was kind and honest, a rock of a man who held her and promised no harm would come to them, and she believed him.

The pressure of his hands on hers as they guided *Sundance* through the narrow channel between the headlands felt sure and solid. She turned her head, looked up at him, and smiled, loving the way his eyes crinkled at the corners, the way the corners of his mouth lifted, as he smiled back.

The water in the cove was calm, the low sun sending golden shafts of light across the aquamarine sea. Jensen cut the engine so that the only sound was the lap of the ripples against the hull and then the splash of the anchor.

Beth didn't want to move. She wanted to hold onto this moment for as long as possible, the warmth of Jensen's body pressed against the length of her back and thighs, the feel of his steady breath brushing against her cheek. He lifted her hands from the wheel, folding them in his. Her breathing became shallow, her heartbeat loud in her ears. He brought his hands to her collarbones, his thumbs brushing along them, and then stopping over the point where she could feel her pulse racing at her throat.

He made a sound that sounded like a soft groan. 'Oh, Beth,' he muttered, 'have you any idea what you're doing to me?'

She twisted in his arms, pulling her hands free and she thought she saw that flash of anxiety, or perhaps doubt, in his eyes again, but she put her hands flat against his chest, the roughness of the hair there deliciously abrasive against her palms.

'No, Jensen,' she whispered, finding a boldness that she didn't recognise as belonging to her. 'I don't think I do. Would you like to show me?'

It felt like long minutes before he reacted. His

dark eyes, serious and deep, roamed over her face, as if he was trying to commit it to his memory. They returned, to meet her own gaze, with an intensity that rocked her to the core. An overwhelming sensation, which she dimly acknowledged as desire, swept through her, carrying all reason away with it. She needed him to hold her and kiss her. That was all she knew.

He bent and brushed his mouth across her forehead, but that wasn't ever going to be enough. Somehow, without her knowing how, her hands found their way around the back of his neck, her fingers burying themselves in his hair. This was so easy, she thought, when you didn't resist it.

The first touch of his mouth on hers felt like something she'd been waiting for all her life. She sighed and he moved away, his lips hovering a whisper from hers, his eyes searching her face for something.

'Beth,' he murmured. 'Are you sure? Do you want this?'

Her answer was to draw his head down towards her. This time there was no hesitation from either of them. Their lips fused and the force of the emotions that took hold of her was irresistible. Beth gave in to them, feeling herself pulled into a vortex of need and exquisite sensation and not caring where it took her.

His lips moved gently, coaxing her, lifting briefly to utter a whispered 'yes' as he changed the angle of his mouth, before returning, this time with more pressure, urging her silently to open to him. When she did, a moan of pleasure sounding deep in her throat, the exquisite warmth of the tip of his tongue stroking across her lips sending a jolt of sensation so pure and elemental through her body, she gripped his shoulders and cried out.

'I'm sorry, Beth. Are you all right? Do you want to stop?'

'Don't stop. Please.'

After that he seemed to hold back a little, his kiss deepening slowly, thoroughly, his tongue, just a flicker at first, becoming bolder and exploring every part of her mouth, urging her to do the same for him. One hand slid around the back of her neck, his strong fingers cupping her head, while the other moved in long strokes down her spine, finally resting in the small of her back.

She hesitated at first, unsure, but his gentle encouragement reassured her and then his taste, his warmth, the closeness of it, were so new and exciting that she craved more and more, fusing her body to his, longing to feel his touch all over her, lost in the sheer magic of it.

When it ended, and they pulled apart, breathless, he laid her head on his chest, brushing her hair from her forehead. His heartbeat was quick and strong under her cheek, his breathing ragged. He smoothed a hand over her shoulder blades, holding her to him and she didn't want him to let her go. She looped her arms around his waist, leaning against him, limp and spent.

'Let me take you home,' he whispered. 'It's been the best of days. Thank you.'

CHAPTER TEN

WHEN JENSEN WOKE, he rolled onto his back, throwing a crooked arm across his face to block out the slanting rays of the morning sun. Thoughts of Beth ambushed him and he groaned. Her scent still lingered in his senses, the taste of her skin on his lips and tongue. The memory of the way she'd moved her mouth against his, pleading wordlessly for more, sent renewed heat barrelling through him.

Would she have stayed if he'd asked her? A part of him hoped not. It would have been too much, too soon, but now he wished she were here, in his arms.

It was a long time since he'd experienced anything approaching happiness and he explored the unfamiliar emotion carefully. In Beth's company he felt deep contentment, and now, added to that, electrifying desire. He'd tried to convince himself that it was because he hadn't had female company— *had sex*—for so long, but deep down he knew this was more complicated than that.

Their conversations had never touched on previous relationships, but he couldn't believe that a woman like her hadn't had any. He wanted her, and she'd shown how much she wanted him. It should be simple.

He could offer her nothing. His life lay behind him, destroyed, his reputation in tatters. While he'd begun to move forward, while he worked at putting *Sundance* back in order, he was only at the very beginning. The future was still a foreign country through which he'd have to try to navigate a route. Sometimes it felt like a nightmare, sometimes like a devilish game for which the rules had been torn up.

Beth did not need someone like him in her life, holding her back, weighing her down with his own baggage.

Her life had been torn apart, but she had the strength and courage to see positivity in the ruins. She seemed to share the values he'd always stood for—honesty, integrity and truth—and circumstances had conspired to rip up those principles, forcing her to take stock, try to work out how to rebuild a life from the fragments left to her.

His presence in her life could be the last thing she needed, but what if he asked her for help? He'd been hell-bent on doing this on his own. He'd cut himself off from the world, certain that nobody wanted to be associated with him, but she'd shown him something different. With her, he could be the best version of himself and he hadn't been that for more years than he cared to remember. He thought she trusted him, and he could feel himself beginning to trust her, too. What if he could build on that trust and learn to stop running and begin to build something solid in his life again?

Going below, he splashed cold water on his face and rubbed a towel over his jaw. Then, studying his reflection in the mirror above the basin, he made a decision. It was time he stopped hiding from himself, as well as the rest of the world.

It was mid-afternoon by the time he leapt out of the RIB and crossed the beach. He felt energised. As he climbed the path to the villa, he wondered how he would find Beth today. Had she slept well, woken refreshed and enjoyed the quiet routine of her day so far?

When she woke, had she thought about him and the magical day they'd spent together, ending in that spectacular embrace?

He'd taken her ashore last night and they'd walked up through the trees to the villa hand in hand. It had felt as natural as breathing. But at the door he'd simply brushed his lips against her forehead and turned away. Any more than that and he would never have left. His body had sung with desire and anticipation, but he'd walked away.

Had she tossed and turned in her bed, as he

had on his mat on the deck of *Sundance*, thinking, wondering, what it could have been like?

She was stretched out on a sunbed, in her red bikini, reading.

'Beth?'

He hadn't startled her. She lowered the book and turned her head towards him, as if she'd been expecting him. He crossed the grass to the terrace and stood looking down at her. She hadn't reached for her towel or beach wrap to cover herself. His hungry eyes devoured her, moving from her hair, which was loosely caught on top of her head, exposing the slender curve of her neck, down to the tips of her toes.

The red bikini moulded to her shape, accentuating the curve of her hips and breasts, the dip of her waist. His mouth went dry.

Her pale golden skin gleamed and there was a bottle of sunscreen lying on the tiles beside her.

'Jensen.'

He dragged his attention back to reality and tried to smile. 'I could do your back if you'd like.'

She looked at him and sat up, swinging her feet to the ground, pushing her sunglasses onto the top of her head.

'You've…changed?'

He spiked his fingers through his hair, still surprised by its new, shorter length.

'I've been to the barber in the village. A Turkish barber, in Turkey.' He smiled down at her.

Beth stood and raised a hand and her fingers hovered at his cheek before brushing lightly across his smooth jaw.

'You look different, and yet the same.'

'Do you mind?' He thought she looked faintly bemused.

'Mind? Of course not. Although I quite liked the stubble…' Her forehead creased and she studied him through narrowed eyes. 'You just remind me…no, sorry. Ignore me.' She shook her head. 'It's nothing.'

He reached up for her hand and tugged her towards him until they were almost touching. Almost. She lifted her face and he took it in both hands to kiss her.

It was everything he remembered from yesterday, and more. He loved the feeling of his newly shaved skin against her soft cheek. He imagined how it would feel against the satiny skin of her abdomen. Her thighs. His tee shirt and the red triangles of fabric that were her bikini top and bottom felt like a flimsy barrier between them, and yet getting past them felt impossible.

He didn't dare to close the gap but with a small, impeded sound, Beth pressed her body against his, her hands running down his back and then up under the hem of his tee shirt to spread across his shoulders. He had a brief, vivid memory of the feeling of her hands rubbing the sunscreen onto his back yesterday before his mind narrowed and all his blood went south. His focus shrank to the point of what was happening right here, right now.

She pulled away from his mouth, breathing hard. 'Jensen. I think I...want you.'

He ran his hands down her arms, taking her hands in his and bringing them up to cup them against his chest. His forehead rested on hers.

'I want you, too, Beth. So much. But that's not why I came.'

'Why, then?'

'I came to ask you to dinner. Will you come out with me, on a date?'

'A date?'

'Yes. You know, when two people agree to go out together. It's called a date.'

'I... Jensen, this isn't a teasing matter. I know what a date is. I just don't know where we'd go on one round here.' She looked around. 'Unless it's to the café in the village, but I don't know how late they stay open. Or perhaps you're going to cook me dinner on *Sundance*?'

'It's more special than that.'

'More special than *Sundance*? Impossible.'

'There's a village up the coast where the little restaurant in the harbour has a big reputation. The only reason it's not packed every night is because it's only accessible by boat.'

'So we're going on our date on *Sundance*.'

'The sea is going to be like glass this evening. It'll take twenty minutes in the RIB.'

'Are you sure?'

'Positive. You won't even get your feet wet. That is, if you say yes.'

'If I say yes, will you tell me what made you get your hair cut and a proper shave?'

'I promise.'

'Yes, then, I'll come. I'm eaten up with curiosity.'

'Be on the beach at six. I'll pick you up.'

Beth showered and washed her hair. She dried it in shiny waves and carefully smoothed some pink lipstick onto her mouth and a hint of eyeshadow to her eyelids. Of the three dresses she'd brought with her, she chose the one Jensen hadn't seen. It had a row of tiny mother-of-pearl buttons down the front, from the deep vee neck to below the waist, and the pale lavender cotton fell in soft pleats from the dropped waist and swirled in soft folds around her calves. She added a spritz of perfume. A restaurant, however big its reputation, could not be too formal if all its clientele arrived by boat, she told herself.

Half an hour later, as they motored into the tiny harbour and found a place to tie up at the quay, she realised that depended entirely on the kind of boat.

Several superyachts were anchored in the bay,

the owners evidently ferried ashore by their skippers in sleek, gleaming speedboats, which now bumped together gently alongside the pontoons.

'Will we get a table?' She hooked a hand through Jensen's arm, feeling suddenly unsure.

'I asked Omer at the village shop to call them this morning to make a reservation.'

'Oh. So you planned this. And you were confident I'd agree to come on a date with you.'

'Not confident. Hopeful.'

Their table was tucked away at the end of the terrace with a view over the harbour. Candlelight flickered in a glass lantern on the blue-checked tablecloth. The darkening water reflected the last of the sunset and as lights came on around the edge of the bay and on the yachts anchored further out, the scene took on a dreamlike quality.

'Thank you for bringing me here, Jensen. It's magical.'

'How would you rate your date, so far?'

'A perfect ten. I can't see how it could get any better.'

Jensen took her hand, brushing his thumb across her knuckles. 'Want to bet?'

'You'd lose.'

His thumb moved to trace a light circle on her palm. 'I don't think so.'

The food was simple and exquisite, with fish as fresh as it could be, buttery little potatoes and crunchy salad. The wine Jensen chose from the small list tasted like honey and sunshine on her tongue.

Beth settled back in her chair. 'I think that counts as a perfect meal. These little pastries are sinfully good.' She licked her fingers. 'There's only one thing you still need to do.'

'Oh?'

'Mmm. Tell me what happened to the pirate I sailed away with, yesterday?'

Jensen propped his folded arms on the table and nodded. He looked out over the small harbour, then back at her. His eyes had lost their navy in the dim light and turned almost black.

'Yeah. I did say I would. I thought you might have forgotten.'

'No.' Beth smoothed the skirt of her dress over her thighs, sensing his hesitation. 'But if it's something you don't want to discuss, that's fine, too.'

'I've been…stuck,' he began, slowly. He dropped his eyes to the table, lifting his shoulders, then he dropped them and looked directly at her. 'I thought when I got to where I was going, I'd feel different. Unburdened. That I'd be able to come to terms with things, make a plan and move ahead with my life in a direction of my own choice. Rather like you.'

'I…'

He held up a hand, broad palm facing her. She wanted to wrap her fingers around his and hold him, but she kept her hands in her lap, aware that he needed to speak without distraction.

'I thought my head would be clear and I'd be able to think, but I couldn't. Things caught up with me and held me back. I couldn't shake them off. I wanted to be on my own, but you were there. Then I wanted to spend time with you, but I resented that want. It wasn't how things were meant to be.'

'I felt much the same at first. I wanted you gone. You've fixed *Sundance*, so I suppose you will be, soon. Only now...' She swallowed, emotion clogging her throat. 'Is that what you were going to tell me? That you're ready to go?'

'Not at all. I think what I'm trying to say is that I'm ready to stop; to stop trying to outrun my life. When you said that thing about the journey only just beginning, it made so much sense to me. I thought I was at the end of it, and I couldn't figure out why I didn't feel better. Accepting that this is just the beginning somehow set my mind free. Yesterday, with you,' he said, reaching across the table and pulling one of her hands from her lap, enclosing it in his, 'was the best day of my life. Seeing how you opened up and enjoyed it made me so...*happy*. And the way we kissed was...' His inbreath was shaky. 'It was beyond words. I wanted you. And when I woke this morning, I wished I'd asked you to stay.'

'I didn't mind that you took me home. I knew you'd come back. I was happy to wait for you.'

'But this morning I also thought about how far I still have to go, and whether I'll ever feel worthy of someone like you. And I wondered if you might be able to…help.'

Beth felt tears prick her eyes. She blinked them away. She could only imagine how difficult it was for Jensen, a strong, independent, self-reliant man, to ask anyone for help. He was used to solving problems, making things work, finding a way, and yet he'd stalled, held back by whatever it was that had happened to him. He needed her help, not her pity.

'I'm honoured,' she said, lightly, 'that you've asked, and of course I'll help, if I can, but you still haven't told me why…'

He released her hand and sat back, running his fingers through his hair. 'I was coming to that. I decided that a good start would be to stop hiding behind my appearance. If I'm to get anything of my life back, it must not be as a man badly disguised as a pirate.'

'Okay. I get that. But I think, if I'm going to be of any practical help to you, I need to know more about your past.'

His beautifully curved mouth, until this morning hidden from her behind his scruff, flattened into a straight line, the lips she'd been thinking about kissing again, all evening, thinned. He shook his head and pressed his fingers to his temples.

'I don't think I'm ready for that.'

CHAPTER ELEVEN

AT FIRST THE moon was just a pale smudge of light on the horizon but within minutes it had hauled itself out of the sea to sail free in the night sky, leaving a silver wake across the water.

'It was the perfect setting for a date, with perfect food and wine. Did you order the moon, too?'

'I might have tried.' With his hand on the tiller, Jensen guided the RIB between the headlands. The low lights he'd left burning on *Sundance* glowed invitingly. He slowed the engine to a throb so that the craft rode quietly on the still waters of the cove. 'Since it has appeared on cue, how do you feel about rounding off our date with a moonlight swim?'

'Have you been planning that, too? All part of the perfect evening?'

'You bet me it couldn't get any better. Remember?'

'Mmm. I do. It sounds like an amazing idea, but I think my bet is safe. I don't have my bikini or swimsuit with me.'

He opened the throttle a little and guided the RIB to the platform at *Sundance*'s stern.

'If I'd planned it, I would have suggested you bring them with you. I could lend you a tee shirt. If you like.'

In the light from the cockpit just above them, Jensen watched conflicting emotions chase across her face. Her growing, but still fragile confidence wanted to say yes, he was sure, but her insecurities were urging her to refuse. If sailing had been out of her comfort zone, then swimming with him in the moonlight would be on a whole different level.

He moored the RIB securely to *Sundance*, busying himself with the few things that needed to be done to make it safe, deliberately not meeting Beth's gaze or pressing her for an answer. Standing up, with one hand on the platform to keep them steady, he held out the other to her, helping her to step across.

He heard her inhale deeply and then breathe out.

'Yes.' She probably didn't sound as positive as she'd hoped.

'Okay.' He kept his voice light. 'You can change your mind if you want to. It's allowed.'

'I don't want to change my mind, but the idea does make me anxious. A week ago, a moonlight swim would have been so far out of my usual range of experience... I can't believe I'm even contemplating it.'

'Shall I get a tee shirt? While you think about it?'

There was a brief silence and he turned to look at her. She nodded. 'Yes, please. But I think you'd better hurry, in case I change my mind, after all.'

'That'll be fine, too. There's no pressure. It's meant to be fun. Come up on deck. There's a ladder down the side. It's the safest way to get into the water.'

Jensen handed her a tee shirt through the hatch and disappeared. 'I'm going to change,' he called from below.

Beth undid the buttons of her dress with shaking fingers and slipped it off her shoulders, quickly pulling Jensen's tee shirt over her head. Her courage failed her when she thought about removing her underwear, so she kept it on. Was this, she thought, the most foolish thing she'd ever done? It was so out of character for her that she wondered if her senses had been corrupted by the exoticism of the whole evening.

Mentally, she corrected herself. It was out of character for the old Beth: the one who never did anything new, or challenging. For her remaining time in Turkey she would be the new, best version of herself, who seized opportunities to test her courage and made the most of this fragile, exquisite bubble of happiness in which she found herself, in Jensen's company.

She stepped out of the pool of lavender cotton at her feet as Jensen emerged from below decks, wearing his board shorts.

'Still up for this? You don't have to, you know.'

Beth nodded, afraid that her voice might give away just how nervous she felt. It's just a swim, she told herself. You're a good swimmer. No, it's not, her old voice reminded her. It's a swim, in the sea, in the moonlight.

With a rugged, handsome, caring man who had kissed her with reverence, as if she was the most precious thing he'd ever held.

She watched him swing himself over the rail, onto the ladder. Seconds later she heard the soft splash as he entered the water.

Taking a deep breath, she followed him.

He was waiting for her at the bottom of the ladder. The water was silky against her skin as she sank into it. It was cool but the gasp she gave was from pleasure rather than cold.

'Oh, this is…exquisite.' She turned, finding Jensen close behind her. 'It's the most incredible feeling.'

She swam a few strokes, then stopped, suddenly anxious about moving too far from *Sundance*.

'I'll stay close to you, Beth. You must get out as soon as you feel cold.'

Beth rolled onto her back, gazing up into the

velvet depths of the starred sky, feeling her body supported and held by the water.

They swam together around *Sundance*, crossing the path of moonlight that stretched across the bay and turned their limbs silver, and the drops of water they splashed into glittering crystals.

'I think we should probably get out now, before the cold sets in.' Jensen put a hand in the small of her back, urging her towards the ladder. 'If you love it so much we can always do it again, another night.'

'Yes, but it'll never be like this again. I think I've lost the bet.' She turned towards him, laughing, and wrapped her legs around his waist.

'Beth…no.' He seized her hands and held them against his chest, as if he needed to stop them from touching him anywhere else. 'I need…we need to get out.'

A sudden breeze ruffled the surface of the water as they climbed the ladder. Back on the deck, Beth shivered.

Jensen picked up one of the towels he'd brought out and wrapped it around her shoulders.

'Come on. A hot shower will warm you up.' He pushed her gently towards the hatch and helped her onto the ladder.

She glanced over her shoulder. 'My dress…'

'I'll get it for you in a minute.'

The shower in the en suite bathroom was the

more spacious, so he ushered her towards it, opening the door. Her teeth chattered and he swore under his breath. This had been reckless. Seeing Beth face challenges and overcome anxieties was hugely rewarding but now he felt he had pushed her too far. She was cold and probably mildly shocked. He reached into the shower, turning on the water and adjusting the temperature.

Beth stood shivering, clutching the towel at her neck. 'I'm n...not cold. I'm just...' Another bout of shivering blurred her words.

Jensen prised the towel out of her fists and dropped it on the floor. He gripped the hem of the sodden tee shirt and lifted it over her head. Even though he knew he had to get her into the hot shower and warmed up as fast as possible, he stopped, the tee shirt hanging from one hand, his breath caught in his throat, as he gazed at her.

Why had he thought she'd wear sensible underwear?

The wet, lacy garments enhanced rather than hid her nakedness, holding her perfect, rounded breasts captive and defining the vee at the apex of her thighs.

Her name was a groan in his throat as he put his hands on her hips and guided her under the steaming spray.

She tilted her head back and gasped, then twined her arms around his neck and pulled him towards her.

He pressed his cheek to the top of her head, sliding his fingers under the thin straps that ran over her shoulders.

'Beth...are you sure?'

'I've never been more sure...of anything,' she whispered as his mouth found hers.

His hands cupped her face as he kissed her, exploring her lips and mouth with slow thoroughness, then letting his mouth follow his hands, over the frantic pulse at her neck, down to the ivory and pink perfect orbs of her breasts, and on to her curved hips, hooking his fingers into the lacy thong and dispensing with it.

He felt her tug at the waistband of his shorts, and he eased them over his hips, kicking them out of the way. Then he wrapped his arms around her and held her still, loving the feel of her body pressed against the length of his and feeling like a man who'd been dying of thirst finding an oasis of sweet water in the desert.

He turned off the water and wrapped her in the robe that hung by the door, and carried her out into the cabin, setting her down and slipping the fluffy fabric from her shoulders, drinking in the sight of her as he laid her on the wide bed and covered her body with his.

CHAPTER TWELVE

'I'M SORRY.' Jensen's fingers traced over her cheek and jaw. His voice and the kiss he gave her were soft but the hard, bunched muscles of his shoulders, under her hands, told her he wasn't relaxed, at all.

'What for?'

He rested his face in the hollow of her shoulder. 'That wasn't the best…it's been a while.'

Beth smoothed her hands over the hard planes of his back, feeling his muscles shiver. 'For me it was perfect.'

'Next time…'

'There'll be a next time?' She spiked the fingers of one hand into his hair, massaging the base of his skull, while the other traced feather-light circles in the small of his back.

He lifted his head and smiled against her mouth.

'All too soon, if you carry on doing that. I'm not *that* old.'

'Mmm.' She increased the pressure, surprising herself, again, at how easy it was to be with him. Everything felt as if it was meant to be. There had been no self-consciousness or awkwardness. 'Promise?' She shifted beneath him, hooking a leg over the back of his thigh.

'Can you...keep still?' He cradled her face between his hands and kissed her. 'Just for...a minute?'

'No. I...'

'Beth.'

Eventually, they slept. Beth woke in the dawn half-light with the weight of an arm across her waist.

She turned her head carefully to look at Jensen. His expression was peaceful, his breathing quiet. He moved his head a little; his profile, clear and unblurred, was etched against the light creeping into the porthole beyond.

Something in Beth's brain clicked into place. She blinked, but he'd moved, and the memory slipped. She turned over and he tightened his arm, pulling her into the curve of his body and resting his chin on her head. She thought he murmured her name. She slept again.

Jensen slipped out of the master cabin. He pulled on an old pair of shorts, made himself a strong cup of his favourite coffee and carried it up onto the foredeck.

It was the best time of day. The sun had just risen above the horizon and the air still felt cool, the only sounds the creaking of *Sundance*'s rigging and the quiet slap and suck of water against her hull. A seabird swooped low over the water on silent wings.

He slid down onto the deck, leaning his back against the mast. It was the first time he'd slept indoors for weeks. In Beth's arms he had forgotten how intolerable he found sleeping in an enclosed space. She'd still been deeply asleep when he'd woken, and he hadn't wanted to disturb her, just yet.

The magnetic attraction between them had been there from the start, although he had denied it. He smiled as he remembered how they had tried to avoid one another; the rules they'd—*he'd*—laid out about using the beach, protecting their privacy, giving each other as wide a berth as possible.

None of it had worked. They'd been drawn together and now it seemed that every second they'd spent in each other's company had led, inexorably, to the bed, where Beth now slept, below the deck, and the unfathomable joy that she had given him, and, he hoped, he had given her.

Apart from joy, she'd given him something else. A flame of hope flickered in his heart. She made him believe that things could change for him and would be different from now on, as they opened their hearts to one another. The certain knowledge that he was a different person—a better man—when he was with her made that hope grow stronger by the second.

He could hardly wait for her to wake so he could tell her how he felt.

When Beth next woke, Jensen was gone. She put out a hand and found his pillow was cool, in the indent where his head had lain. She felt bereft, still feeling the imprint of his body along her back and thighs.

She listened for signs that he might be moving about in the galley, or in the shower, but there were none. She'd expected to wake, slowly, and find herself still cocooned in his arms. She just couldn't imagine being anywhere else, right now.

Then she remembered the quick snapshot her brain had called up in the early hours of the morning. It had lasted half a second and then vanished but now that she'd thought about it again, it persisted.

She pushed herself upright, more detail added to the memory as sleep receded. Apprehension propelled her out of bed. She pulled on the soft robe in which Jensen had wrapped her after their shower, only to slide it off her again minutes later, before lifting her onto the bed. Wrapping it around herself, she padded towards the galley.

A faint smell of coffee hung in the air and the sky was a square of pale blue morning light, through the open hatch at the top of the companionway.

Jensen was not in the cockpit. Perhaps he'd gone for an early morning swim, but there was no sign of him in the waters around *Sundance* as she climbed up to the deck and worked her way forward, towards the bow.

He was almost hidden by the foremast, but she could see his bare, bronzed feet on the deck, his elbows resting on his drawn-up knees. His big hands were wrapped around a coffee mug. Last night she'd discovered how those slightly rough hands, which were adept at fixing so many things, were also capable of infinite gentleness, and of eliciting undreamt-of pleasure from her body. As she approached, she could see he was resting his head against the timber mast, his gaze fixed on something distant.

She watched him for a long moment, sharply aware that she stood at a crossroads, making an agonising choice. She badly wanted to retreat softly, slide back into bed and wait for him to return to her. She need say nothing.

But Beth knew, even before she'd formed the thought, that she could not go down that path. Jensen deserved her honesty; of that she was certain. It might destroy the fragile beginning of something beautiful and precious, but it might also make it stronger. Whatever happened, she could not deceive him.

Sucking in a deep breath, she stepped forward. 'JJ?'

The quick twist of his head as he turned to stare at her was all the confirmation she needed.

She was right.

She'd asked him to take her back to bed, but he'd refused. Instead, he'd made her a mug of coffee and brought it up onto the deck for her.

'You didn't drink yours, Jensen. It's cold.'

He shrugged, resumed his place in front of the mast, and patted the deck beside him.

But Beth positioned herself between his knees, shuffling backwards until she could lean against his chest, cradling the warm mug in her hands. Jensen combed his fingers through her hair, teasing out some of the tangled evidence of their night of lovemaking. 'How long have you known?' he asked, after a long silence.

She reached up and stilled his hand in its restless caressing of her hair. 'Since early this morning, although yesterday, when you'd been to the barber, something...' She sipped the coffee. 'This morning, I glimpsed the outline of your profile in a particular light, not blurred by that stubbly beard and long hair, and it jogged a memory.'

'I tried to avoid the press.'

'You did well. In the few pictures I saw, you'd shielded your face. But there was one...'

'Yes, I know.' He dragged a hand over his face, shaking his head. 'It was the day I was sentenced.'

Beth put her coffee on the deck and reached for his hands with both of hers. He let her take them and she pulled his arms over her shoulders and kissed his knuckles, settling against his chest again.

'I'm sorry.' Her voice was husky. 'It must have been dreadful.'

He took a couple of breaths, hoping to control the shake in his voice. 'I didn't know it was possible to feel—*to be*—so helpless. You know you're innocent; that you've done nothing—*nothing*—wrong, but twelve strangers decide you're lying. And there is nothing…*nothing*…you can do about it.'

He stirred, needing to move, unable to keep still and remember, but Beth kept him anchored against her.

'But now you're free and declared innocent.'

'I'm free, yes, from prison. But I'll never be free of the stigma of having been there. That's not something anyone is going to forget.'

'Your friends and family must have believed in you, though. And they've been vindicated.'

Jensen laughed, but even he recognised the harshness in the sound. 'Someone like you, Beth, with your loyalty and honesty, might find it hard to imagine how quickly friends, and even family, will put a safe distance between themselves and disgrace.'

She twisted her head and looked up at him, her expression of shock confirming his words.

'Your *family*?'

'Yup. My wife—'

'Wife?' Shock jolted through her. 'Jensen—'

'*Ex*-wife. And my daughter. I haven't heard from them, since.'

'You have a daughter?'

He nodded. 'Emily. She's fifteen. And beautiful. I…' In spite of his iron control, his voice broke.

'But it was declared a miscarriage of justice. Surely now they'll…'

He rolled his head against the mast, liking the sense of solidity and permanence it gave him. 'Even if they did, would I want them in my life again, when they'd believed I was guilty of stealing from a children's charity?'

'No. But your daughter is at an impressionable age. She must have been influenced by what other people said. She's not old enough to have made a sound judgement. She'll want to be a part of your life now. And your friends…'

'One friend. James and I go way back. He's a lawyer. He wouldn't accept the judgement and he made it his mission to expose the truth. It's thanks to him that I'm free.'

'What a good friend. You must have had quite a celebration with him when you were released.'

Jensen closed his eyes, forcing himself to think about those first hours and days of freedom.

'No,' he said, feeling tightness in his throat. 'When I was released, I went to my apartment to collect a few things and then I went straight to Heathrow Airport. I didn't see or speak to anyone except the cab driver and staff at the airport.'

He felt Beth go still.

'But you've spoken to James since? Surely…'

How could he explain that desperate need to be on his own, doing whatever he wanted, after months of regulated prison life, every minute of every day, and some of the nights, regimented and allocated to something or other? There'd been no peace, or quiet.

'No,' he said, eventually. 'I've spoken to nobody. I turned off my phone, let the battery die. You're the only person who knows where I am.'

'But…people…must be worried about you. You should make contact with someone.'

'No one cared about me when I was locked up. Why should they care now?' The familiar taste of bitterness was strong in his mouth.

'James cared. He must be beside himself with worry about you.'

'James knows me, and so he will know that I'll get in touch when I want to. He won't try to find me until I'm ready to be found.'

'Jensen—I don't think I can call you anything else.'

'No, please don't. JJ was my name—Jonathan

Jensen Heath—in *that* life. I'm no longer that person.'

'Could you bear to tell me about that life?' The stroke of her thumbs across his knuckles was soothing. 'I'd like to understand what happened. But if it's too difficult for you, we can wait until another time.'

Jensen's breath quickened, and his heart hammered, at the thought of relating the story. Beth must be able to feel his heartbeat against her back, but she gave no sign. When he'd walked out of the prison gates, a free man, he'd tried to put it behind him.

He hadn't always been successful. But he wanted Beth to know. He didn't want her to have any doubts about him, even though knowing who he was must now have thrown up the biggest doubt in her mind.

The best gift he could give her would be the perfect memory of this time together.

He bent his head and brushed his cheek against hers.

'I made my money—an obscene amount—as a hedge-fund manager. I loved the life, but the stress was insane and I knew if I didn't get out, I would burn out, so I quit while I was ahead. It turned out that my…ex-wife…loved the life, too, and she wasn't ready for the change of pace. She missed it—the parties, the restaurants, the chalets in Gstaad and St Moritz and the helicopter skiing—all the things I liked the least about it.' He shifted his thighs, tightening them around Beth's hips. 'The way I relaxed, once a year, was to take *Sundance* on a sailing trip, but she hated that. In the end we split. She took Emily and married another city high-flier.'

'But you still saw your daughter?'

'Oh, yes, there was no problem about access, especially when she wanted the freedom to go off on a fancy trip somewhere. Emily and I had great times together. I tried to be the best father and I miss her...'

'I'm so sorry.' Beth pressed her mouth against his hands. 'I can't imagine how you must feel.'

'Lonely, regretful, guilty. All those things. And...hurt. It hurts to think Emily believed I was a criminal.'

'I feel sure,' Beth whispered, 'you'll be able to put things right with her. She'll need time, but it'll happen.'

'I wish I shared your confidence. Anyway, I wanted to do something worthwhile with my time, and when the opportunity came up to be the CEO of the charity, it seemed like the perfect solution. I loved the job, but I admit there was a time, during the divorce, when I took my eye off the ball. I wanted to make things as easy as possible for Emily and I lost focus, briefly. That's when it happened.'

'Someone framed you?'

'Essentially, yes. Money disappeared. A lot of

money. As the CEO I was ultimately accountable, but I was astonished by what had happened. I couldn't understand it. I was arrested and the finance guy—the CFO—took over. They appointed one of the most aggressive prosecuting lawyers in the City, and they got their conviction. I'd still be there if it weren't for James' work.'

'He found new evidence?'

Jensen nodded. 'The verdict was overturned, and I was released. The new investigation is ongoing, but I've been out of touch, so I don't know what progress has been made, if any, in identifying the culprit.'

'What did you do when you got to Heathrow?'

'I took the first available flight to Athens. By that night I was in the only place I wanted to be: on *Sundance*. I sailed out of Piraeus the next morning, early. I think you know the rest.'

'Mmm. You sailed alone, with the aim of getting here. That must have been tough.'

'Sometimes. But being free and master of my own destiny again was so mind-blowing, I didn't mind how tough it was. In fact, the times I sailed through the night were the best. When I had to devote all my powers of concentration to the wind, the sails, the sea, it stopped me thinking about anything else. And after a passage like that, I was exhausted enough to sleep.'

'And you got here and found me. What a letdown.'

He almost smiled. 'A surprise, yes. A shock, maybe. But not a let-down, and soon a tentative kind of pleasure.'

'And now?'

'Now?' How could he tell her what he felt now? 'Oh, Beth, I've loved being with you. Seeing you face challenges, overcome anxieties, take delight in new experiences has been transformative for me. It's made me believe that I can have hope. Maybe things can be different. You make me *feel* different because you've made me feel again. I was numb with pain, disbelief, anger, for so long, but you've unlocked something. But...'

'But?'

He tightened his hold on her. 'But now the past has caught up with me...with us. I would have told you eventually, but I wanted you to get to know me better, first. I wanted you to learn to trust me. I hate the thought that you might doubt me, or not believe in me.'

Beth moved away and turned to face him. Their knees touched and she still held onto his hands.

'I need to look at you and hear you say that, and then I need you to explain how this works, Jensen. We enjoy each other's company. I find you so easy to be with and that's a whole new experience for me. And last night...' She stopped and took a breath that stuttered in her throat. 'Last night was more wonderful than I could ever have imagined it would be.'

'Beth...'

'Are you saying you think I'll walk away from that? Because I need to tell you that I don't know how to.'

Her green eyes were huge, her teeth fastened over her soft lower lip and he could see the pulse thrumming at her neck. He wanted to put his mouth there and feel her life force.

'I'm saying that if we don't I'm so afraid of ruining the rest of your life.'

Beth let go of Jensen's hands and scrambled to her feet. The towelling robe swung open and she grabbed the edges of it, wrapping it around herself and tying the belt in a fierce, tight knot.

She stared down at him. 'What do you mean?'

Jensen unfolded himself and stood up, stepping past her. He put his hands on the rail and dropped his head.

There were marks on his back she must have made last night. She wanted to stroke her fingers over them, or touch her lips to them, but she pushed her hands into her pockets, balling her fists.

He straightened, looking out over the sea. The day had started to warm up and Beth would have liked to find some shade, but she felt stuck where she was, waiting for his answer.

At last, he turned, his expression grim and distant.

'I mean,' he said carefully, 'that my reputation for truth, integrity and compassion—everything I believed in—has been destroyed. My life, as I knew it, is in ruins. Even though I've been exonerated of the crime for which I was found guilty, it will take years to cast off the shadow of that conviction and jail term.'

'I don't care…'

He held up a hand to stop her.

'You should. You *must* care, about your own future.' He looked down, then raised his eyes to her face again. 'You have so much potential. You can make your future whatever you want. What you don't want is to be associated with someone like me.'

'What is someone like you meant to be like?'

'Beth, I've lost all credibility. Nobody will want to work with me.'

'So because I now know who you are, you think I won't want to be with you?'

Jensen nodded.

'That's ridiculous. Everything that has happened between us happened before I recognised you.'

'I know, but we can't undo it. Now that you know who I am, you should be running as fast as possible in the opposite direction.'

'Well, I'm not.' Beth slid her hands around his

waist. 'Last night you asked for my help. Well, I'm asking for yours now.' She laid her cheek against his chest, feeling the thud of his heart speed up as she pulled him against her. 'Just please don't do this.'

Jensen's cheek pressed against the crown of her head. His chest rose in a long, slow breath.

'Beth, this is crazy. How can I possibly help you?'

'You can help me to understand what I need to do to support you, Jensen. Meeting you, having you care about me, knowing you enjoy being with me, and wanting to make love to me have been the best things that have ever happened to me. I'm not giving all that up. I'm strong enough to fight for both of us and that is what I'm going to do.'

'Beth, let me take you home. When you have space to think clearly, away from me, you'll realise I'm not worthy of you.' He bracketed her face, stroking his thumbs across her cheekbones. 'You'll have to find somewhere to live, find a new job, rebuild your life. You won't want me...'

She raised her chin. 'I may be a homeless, unemployed, forty-five-year-old woman who doesn't know what the future holds, but for the first time in my life I'm free to make my own choices, and I'm choosing to be with you.'

His next breath shuddered in his chest and then his mouth came down over hers, hard and un-compromising, his tongue probing the seam of her lips until she opened to him with a soft moan in her throat. His kiss was hungry, devouring her mouth like a man starved. Those strong hands held her head still while he plundered her sweetness, sending wave after wave of sensation whipping through her, a flame licking its way along her limbs until a fiery need had been ignited in every cell of her body.

She wondered how she could ever live without this now that she'd tasted it. She'd feel as if half of her were missing, if Jensen took it away from her, the half that had been missing up until she'd met him. He'd rescued her from her life of shrunken horizons and self-imposed boundaries and shown her how to fly free. How could he believe she'd choose to crash back to earth, wounded, alone, without him?

Breathless, her lips bruised and swollen, her heart pounding like a drum, Beth dragged her mouth away from his. 'Jensen, please…'

His breathing was quick and harsh. 'I'm sorry. I've hurt you. I was rough.'

'No.' She shook her head. 'It's okay. Please,' she pleaded. 'Please take me back to bed.'

Afterwards, Beth couldn't remember how they negotiated the companionway, half falling, in each other's arms, into the galley, or how they stumbled along the passage to the master suite. It was a blur of entangled limbs, kisses that neither of them could stop, and words of need and love, gasped and whispered. He tore the robe from her shoulders. She tugged at his shorts.

Jensen had been gentle before. Now, he made love to her with a desperate urgency, as if he believed it was the last time and he was utterly intent on making every movement, every meeting of lips, every stroke of his clever fingers, one that neither of them would ever be able to forget. Afterwards, as they clung together, drifting in and out of sleep, he raised his head and lifted a strand of her hair, smoothing it away from her forehead, and whispered to her.

'I wish things were different, but I can't wish away what happened to me. Because if none of it had happened, I wouldn't have met you.'

CHAPTER THIRTEEN

JENSEN STOOD UP from the table on Beth's terrace and stretched.

'Thank you for breakfast.' He stacked the plates and cutlery and dropped a kiss onto her head. 'Sun, sea and...'

'Sex?'

His face creased in a smile. 'If you say so. I was going to say surfing. Sun, sea and surfing will work up an appetite.'

'We haven't been surfing, but we have had brilliant...'

'Sex. Yes. You'll wear me out.'

'Actually, I was going to say we've had brilliant times in the sun and the sea, but I'll concede your point. And I don't want to wear you out. What would the point of that be?'

'Then you'd better indulge me this morning.'

'I thought I had, already. More than once.'

Jensen replaced the crockery on the table, took her wrists and pulled her to her feet. 'When last did you wear anything other than your bikini, or nothing?' He dropped her wrists and wrapped his arms around her. 'Not that I'm complaining.'

'Three days ago.' She planted a kiss on his bare chest then rubbed her cheek against his skin. 'I think there're a few more grey hairs here than there were yesterday.'

'Does that surprise you? Like I said, you're wearing me out.'

Beth smiled. 'All right, then, I'll give you a break. How would you like me to indulge you, except in the obvious way?'

'That can come later. Will you come down to the beach this morning?'

'You mean you're willing to share it with me?'

'Since we've shared just about everything else, I think we could give the beach a try.'

'Jensen… I don't think that's a good idea.'

'But you haven't heard my idea yet.' He splayed his hands over her ribcage, running his thumbs along the edge of her bikini top.

She caught her bottom lip in her teeth, hissing in a breath. 'Since you've had a one-track mind for the past three days, I think I can hazard a guess about your idea.'

'Speak for yourself, Beth. And from what I'm seeing, your mind is still running on that same track.' He looked down at the burgeoning triangles of her red bikini top and his attention narrowed and focussed.

She'd gone very still, her breathing deep and

slow. Her body was warm, her curves, which he'd come to know so well, mesmerising. He knew her mouth would taste of the honey she'd had for breakfast, and her hair smelled of lavender and rosemary. Being with her filled him with a depth of happiness he'd never experienced before. She reached his very soul. A while ago he'd thought he'd never smile again, definitely never laugh, but she made him do both, often.

They talked about the past and what had happened to their lives. Somehow, Beth managed to shine a light of positivity onto the darkest of times. She'd lost her job, but looking back, she said, with the perfect vision of hindsight, she could see how stuck, how bound by convention she'd been, in the only job she'd ever had. He thought the edge of bitterness that had sharpened her words when she'd originally spoken about her work had blunted.

She'd lost her home, too, but at least she no longer had to share her space with her toxic stepmother and spoilt stepsister, she said. What could be better than a clean slate? To start afresh?

When she returned to London, she'd have to find a job and all she'd been able to imagine was trying to find one exactly like her old one. Now she felt free, and able to think about looking for something different. Something connected to gardening, which was what gave her joy.

And just because she'd lived all her life in a

large Georgian house in Islington didn't mean she couldn't live somewhere different, as long as she had a garden. Jensen noticed the regret that crept into her voice when she talked about the garden she'd made behind the family home. It was, she said, the one thing she missed from her previous life.

He didn't deserve her. That thought beat a constant refrain in his head, marking time, it seemed, until the moment would be right for it to slide into a discordant cacophony of noise, which he'd be forced to take notice of and act upon. Sometimes it was loud, sometimes an insidious whisper that ambushed him in the dark hours of the early morning, when he looked down at her, asleep in his arms.

He tried to drown out the beat, kissing her awake so he could make love to her again, or swimming, hard and fast, across the bay, pushing himself until his muscles ached and his lungs threatened to burst.

If he didn't deserve her, she sure as hell didn't deserve him, with his prison record, disgraced reputation and a teenaged daughter who hated him. But being with her helped. Very slowly, he was beginning to see a glimmer of light at the end of the tunnel he seemed to have been stuck in for so long.

He dropped his eyes and gazed down at her. Her chest rose and fell slowly, deeply, and her eyelids, fringed with dark lashes, fluttered down over her eyes, her gaze and focus, he knew, turning inwards.

Her fingers traced a pattern across his lower back, but he didn't think she realised she was doing it. She ought to know by now what that did to him. Perhaps she did. Perhaps...

With difficulty, he hauled in a big, deep breath.

'Hey.' Resolutely, he removed his hands from her ribs, feeling goosebumps shiver across her skin as he drew them away.

'Mmm?'

'Come back, Beth, from wherever those thoughts have taken you.'

'Not far,' she murmured. 'Just upstairs...'

'Later. Will you come to the beach in half an hour?'

'Your plan?' Her voice was sleepy, dreamy.

'You'll find out when you get there. And no, it doesn't involve sex on the beach.'

When Beth walked onto the beach thirty minutes later, Jensen was already there. Just above the waterline lay a bright blue windsurfer board and he was engrossed in setting up the sail.

'What are you doing?'

He glanced up. 'Sorting this out. Want to have a go?'

Beth frowned and nudged the board with a foot. 'Where did you get it?'

'It was strapped to the deck on *Sundance*. Hadn't you noticed?'

'When I'm on the deck of *Sundance* there are other things that I find more distracting. And no, I'm not sure I do want to have a go. I wouldn't know how to begin.'

Jensen put the yellow and red sail down and dropped an arm around her shoulders. 'I haven't noticed that stopping you, lately. You could add windsurfing to the list of things you hadn't tried before.'

She raised her eyebrows at him. 'Such as?'

'Sailing? Swimming in the moonlight?'

'So this is where the surfing, as in sun, sea and…*surfing*…comes in.'

'Precisely. *Now* would you like to have a go? I'll be right there with you. The worst that can happen is that you fall in. Over and over again.'

An hour later, Beth had lost count of how many times she'd toppled off the board to hit the water with a shriek and a splash.

The sea in the cove was warm and calm and falling into it was fun, but not being able to master the technique was infuriating.

'There's not really enough wind,' Jensen called, before diving under the water and surfacing next to her. 'It's like riding a bicycle. Easier to balance if you're moving. Impossible if you're not.'

Beth laughed. 'How diplomatic of you to blame

the conditions rather than my obvious ineptitude.' She rolled onto her back, floating, squinting against the sun. 'But it's the most fun I've had since…'

'Since?' His eyes narrowed.

'Well, I was going to say since you let me take the wheel when we were sailing *Sundance* back from Kekova, but then I remembered…'

'This morning, right? And last night, and…' He ducked below the surface as Beth's hand sent a shower of sparkling drops arcing in his direction, then came up behind her.

'Then I remembered the evening we spent at that restaurant up the coast. It was *so* much fun.'

'Mmm.' His voice hummed low in her ear. She turned, about to splash him again, but his dark gaze captured hers and she stilled, watching, as his eyes travelled down her body. His arms slipped around her waist and he pulled her closer. She wrapped her legs around him, gripping his hips.

She felt his fingers move over her back and stop at the clasp of her bikini top.

'Jensen,' she murmured, thinking that drowning in the deep pools of his eyes was a real possibility, 'you said your plan did not include sex.'

'Incorrect, Beth. Try to pay attention.' His breath was warm across her cheek. 'I said it did not involve sex on the beach.'

'So…' She gasped as her top floated free and

his hands splayed over her ribcage, his thumbs teasing her skin.

'So look around and you'll see that this isn't the beach.' His lips hovered a fraction away from hers. 'It's the sea.'

Later, they lay on their backs in the sun, loose-limbed, their hands linked.

'Beth?'

'Mmm?'

'I need to go into the village this afternoon. Omer promised to find me some nylon rope to replace one of the downhauls on *Sundance*. It's one of the last repairs I have to do.' He lifted her hand and kissed the palm. 'Shall I bring back dinner?'

Beth yawned and rolled onto her stomach, propping her chin on her hands. 'What shall we have?'

'Kebabs?'

'Sounds perfect. I'm easily persuaded.'

'I know.' Jensen bent up his legs and propped himself up on his elbows.

'Don't be presumptuous. One day I'll say no.'

'Really?' He ran a finger up her spine, watching how her back arched and her head lifted. 'I'll consider making you change your mind a challenge. We could take bets on how long it would take.'

Beth shook her head. 'I've given up gambling. I lost the last bet.'

'You did. Big time.'

She laughed. 'It was a bet worth losing.'

'I'm glad you think so.'

'I'm sorry I wasn't better at windsurfing. Perhaps it was the teaching.'

Jensen sat up. 'I taught my daughter. She did really well, so I don't think so.'

Beth let the silence stretch. She'd been hoping he'd talk about his daughter, but she'd wanted it to come from him. She'd resisted the urge to raise the subject herself.

Then she reached over and clasped his hand softly in hers. 'How old was she? When you taught her?'

'Seven. We were on holiday in Crete and I hired a special small board for her. She could swim like a fish by the time she was four, and she'd been begging me to let her have a go. She was always so daring and quick to learn.' He shook his head. 'I thought she'd disappear over the horizon. I panicked. But she came back, asking me why I was being so slow.'

'She sounds like you. Is she?'

'She…well, I haven't seen her for a while, so I don't really know now. But she was.' He turned towards her, tracing a circle on her palm with his thumb. That hurt and doubt was in his eyes. 'I think she'd have liked to stay with me, after the divorce, but my lifestyle made it difficult. At least I saw her often, until…'

'Until you were accused.'

'Yes. After that, her mother wouldn't let me near her. She said her schoolfriends would drop her if they knew. But they must have known anyway. It all became very messy and public.'

'Did she want to see you?'

'I don't know. I hate to think she believed I was guilty.'

'You don't know that she did.'

He frowned, propping his head on a hand. 'She must have, obviously.'

'No. She might have believed fiercely that you were innocent. Little girls love their fathers. She might have been utterly loyal. And now that you're a free, innocent man, her mother can't object to her seeing you. She might be desperate to hear from you.'

'I feel afraid to try to contact her. What if she doesn't respond?'

Although Beth hated that he feared contacting his daughter, hearing him admit to his fear made Beth's heart sing.

'You'll never know if you don't try, Jensen. And it seems to me to be a terrible waste of a relationship. It's absolutely worth fighting for. You have a daughter—your own family. Don't let that slip from your grasp because you're afraid of failure.' She squeezed his hand and pulled it towards her, brushing her lips across his fingers. 'I'll give you the Wi-Fi code for the villa. Then if you feel like sending her an email, you can.'

He stood and held out a hand to her and she let him pull her to her feet.

'Will you come back to the villa?'

He shook his head. 'I'll take the windsurfer back out to *Sundance* and then head to the village in the RIB. Would you like me to walk up with you first?'

'No. The quicker you get to and from the village, the quicker you'll be back with me.'

He caught her around the waist and tipped her face up to him with his thumb and forefinger. 'I don't like being parted from you.'

She stretched up on her toes and kissed him lightly. 'Then hurry. I don't like being parted from you either.' She swept an arm out. 'Remember how we had to negotiate with each other about when we'd use the beach, separately?'

'And you didn't keep your side of the bargain.'

'What? I did…'

'No, you didn't. You never came to the beach, even when it was your turn.'

Her forehead creased. 'I didn't like the idea of you watching me from *Sundance*, making sure I didn't overstay my time slot.'

'But if you'd come I would have wanted you to stay longer. I think, even then, I wanted to be with you.'

'When I began to enjoy your company I refused

to admit it, at first. I was determined to want to be on my own. I thought it was what I needed.'

Jensen laughed. 'As we've discovered, we don't always know what's good for us.'

'Oh, I think I do now. And whoever said you can't have too much of a good thing was absolutely right.'

CHAPTER FOURTEEN

BETH SCATTERED CUBES of feta cheese over a plate of sliced tomatoes studded with glistening olives and carried it out to the table on the terrace. 'I'll get the flatbreads. They're warming up in the oven. Oh, those look delicious.'

The smoky aroma of barbecued kebabs rose from the platter Jensen carried towards her. 'Ela made them,' he said. 'All I did was light the barbecue and cook them.'

'We're ready to eat, then.'

'Before we do, could I have that Wi-Fi code?' he asked. 'I've charged my phone. I thought I'd just check my news feed...'

Relief loosened muscles Beth hadn't realised were tense. This was a huge, positive step, but she had to make it feel like something perfectly normal.

She smiled at him, trying to keep her voice light when she replied. 'Of course. It's here somewhere.' She pulled the information file from the bookshelf in the kitchen. 'Second page, I think.'

'Thank you.' He held a smartphone in his hand.

'Are you going to read your emails?'

'Not my emails. There's nobody I want to hear from.'

'What about James?'

'James won't have emailed. He'll wait to hear from me first.'

'Okay.' She pushed the file towards him, across the kitchen island worktop. 'Why don't you go and sit on the terrace while you do that? I'll get the wine.'

She slid the flatbreads, fragrant with warmed spices, from the oven and went to the fridge. She hesitated over choosing the wine, reading one label after the other before finally pulling a bottle of chilled Pinot Grigio from the rack and heading for the door.

Jensen sat with his back to her, an ankle balanced on a knee, one of her favourite poses to see him in. It meant he was comfortable. Relaxed. She paused in the doorway, just to look at him. His broad shoulders in the faded tee shirt, thick dark hair streaked with silver, now neatly cut, long fingers tapping the screen of his phone, all made her heart turn over in her chest.

The feelings he aroused in her were almost too big for her heart to contain. If she weren't holding a cold bottle of wine and a basket of bread, she'd put her arms around his neck and...

'Beth?' He half turned his head, looking over

his shoulder. 'This was a good day to reconnect with the world. It says here that my former CFO has been questioned and the prosecuting lawyer in the case against me, Charles Denby, is being investigated, following an allegation of jury intimidation.'

The bottle of wine slipped from Beth's suddenly nerveless fingers and crashed to the tiles, shattering into a million shards of razor-sharp glass.

Jensen leapt from his chair, causing it to tip over backwards. He dropped his phone, sending it spinning across the table, and swung round. 'What happened? Are you okay?' He took in the wine spreading across the tiles and the jagged pieces of glass. 'Beth, don't move.' He swore beneath his breath. 'Your ankle is bleeding.'

Beth remained motionless, frozen to the spot. Jensen reached out and took the basket of bread from her, putting it on the table. 'Beth?' He glanced around the terrace, looking for something to use to pick up the glass. 'You've gone very white. Do you feel faint?'

She raised her hands to cover her mouth, the movement jerky, and shook her head.

'No.' The word was a hoarse whisper through her fingers. 'No, I don't feel faint. I feel… I'm… *shocked*.'

Jensen relaxed a little. 'It's only a bottle of wine,

Beth. I'm sure there're more in the fridge? Let me clear this up and we'll start again.'

'That's not it.' Her voice shook. 'It was what you said.'

'Something *I* said?' The accident had wiped what he'd said from his mind. He made an effort to think back. It was the news about the CFO and the prosecutor he'd relayed to her. He reached towards his phone.

'My ankle…'

Jensen grabbed a paper napkin from the wire basket on the table and bent to press it against the wound, but Beth took it from his fingers. Gingerly, she raised her foot and rested it on the nearest chair, bending to dab at the injury.

'I said the prosecutor from my case…'

Her hair swung forward, obscuring her face. She pushed it back with one hand. 'You said his… *name*.'

'I did. Let me do that.'

But she shook her head. 'It's okay. Not deep. It was just a shock, hearing his name.'

Jensen's eyes moved from studying her ankle to her face. He drew back a little, moving his feet out of the path of the white wine, which trickled across the floor. He felt confused, struggling to make sense of what had just happened. Their barbecue dinner had been thrown into chaos, but it should be easily fixed. The food was on the table, the glasses ready to be filled. If he could clear up the broken glass and spilled wine, find another bottle, their evening would be restored.

But something had gone wrong; something that was much more fundamental than a broken bottle of wine. He could see it in the expression on Beth's chalk-white face as she straightened up. Incongruously, he noticed that the scattering of freckles across the bridge of her nose stood out in stark contrast to her pallor. She was chewing on her bottom lip, a sure sign of stress.

What was it she'd said?

His name. It was a shock, hearing his name.

Why would a name have shocked her into dropping a bottle of wine?

'I did,' he said, carefully. 'I said his name. Charles Denby.'

Beth released her bottom lip. She folded her arms across her chest and before she buried her hands in her armpits he saw that they were shaking. She raised her chin and stared at him, her gaze unwavering.

'Charles Denby,' she repeated, her voice trembling. She took a breath, noisy and harsh. 'Charles Denby was the prosecutor in your case?'

Jensen nodded and a cold finger of fear snaked up his spine. The happiness he and Beth shared was so fragile. Many things could happen to derail it, but this wasn't one of the ways he'd imagined. He had a sudden image of it being snatched away from them and broken beyond repair, just like the green glass bottle, which lay in dangerous fragments around their feet.

'Yes, he was,' he said, forcing the words out, fearing that once they were out there everything would change, irrevocably. 'Why?'

Beth nodded, once, her chin dropping and then lifting again, higher, as if she was grappling with something, determined to do the right thing, but unsure what that might be. Her shoulders dropped and her spine lengthened as she exhaled and then took a long shaky breath.

'Charles Denby,' she said, her tone flat, devoid of all expression, 'was my boss. He was the reason I left my job.'

He had never had the air punched out of his lungs, but now Jensen thought he knew what it felt like. He tried to breathe, to allow the steady inhalation and exhalation of air to calm him, and his brain to function, but it felt as if there were a great weight pressing onto his chest. That's from the punch, he thought, before remembering there had been no physical blow. Only Beth's words had struck him. He stepped back, but the table behind him dug into his thighs, blocking his retreat. He moved sideways, feeling along its solid edge with his fingertips.

At last his brain, which had seized on the words 'my boss', repeating them over and over again in his head, lurched into action. It hurt to breathe, his heart hammered against his ribs and a clammy chill swept over his skin.

'Did you know?' he asked, quietly, forcing out the words.

'*No.*' The whispered word was barely a breath of sound. 'No, I didn't, Jensen.'

'How could you have worked for him and not known?'

'I'll explain, but I can't do that marooned in a sea of broken glass and sticky spilt wine, with a cut on my ankle.' She gestured to the area around her feet. 'Help me out of this, and then please listen to me.'

He wanted to turn and walk away, but he had to listen to her. He had to know that his sweet, beautiful Beth hadn't been hiding something from him.

He found a brush and dustpan in the cupboard in the laundry. He swept up as much of the glass as he could see, retrieved Beth's flip-flops from beside the sun lounger, and dropped them next to her feet. Then he found the first-aid box and carried it outside, putting it on the end of the table.

He couldn't bear to watch while Beth spread antiseptic ointment over the cut with shaking fingers and stuck on an Elastoplast, remembering how he'd dressed her heel with such care.

Beth closed the lid of the box and walked towards him, but he held up a hand. He didn't want her close. It was too dangerous. She could so easily convince him, with her gentle hands and lips and beguiling scent, that she was telling the truth.

She stopped. 'Jensen, I swear to you that I didn't know. Why wouldn't I have told you?' She pressed the heels of her hands into her eye sockets, rubbing them, and then pulling her palms down over her face. 'Your reaction makes no sense.'

'From my point of view, it's your reaction that makes no sense. And for the record, you are the only thing in my life which has made sense for quite some time.' He pinched the bridge of his nose between a thumb and forefinger.

Beth gripped the edge of the table. 'The man I'd been PA to retired suddenly due to ill health and Charles Denby was brought in to replace him. He was seconded from the New York office.' She pulled out a chair and sat down. 'Please sit down, Jensen. It'll make it easier to talk.'

Slowly, he skirted the table and pulled out the chair opposite her, sitting down and leaning forwards.

'Go on.'

'I heard he made unreasonable demands, but he came with an impressive track record.'

'Huh. Mostly achieved through dubious practices.'

'Maybe.'

'*Maybe?* He's the one being investigated, right?'

She pressed her fingers to her temples. 'You said I should go on. May I?'

'Please do.'

'I was assigned as his PA partly because he was replacing the man I worked for, and partly— I suspect mostly—because I had a reputation for being able to manage difficult people.' She ran her fingers through her thick hair, to the tips, and let it fall around her shoulders. 'A talent which doesn't necessarily make for an easy life.'

He watched her hair tumble to her shoulders and anguish twisted around his heart. He loved that she'd stopped pinning it up in tidy, restrictive styles. He loved feeling the weight of it in his hands, and the way it swung so freely around her shoulders when she walked.

'When was this?'

'It was over a year ago. After your case had been heard. I vaguely knew about it, from the press, but to be honest I hadn't taken much interest in it. My stepmother was ill and I was juggling a lot of things, between home and work. Then she was moved to a care home, and I had more time…' She pushed a lock of hair off her forehead. 'I became aware that he…noticed me. He noticed me in a way I wasn't used to. A way other men never had. For the first time in for ever I didn't have to rush home to care for my stepmother or cook dinner. My stepsister had moved into her own place and took very little notice of her mother.' She inhaled, her breath stuttering.

'Beth,' he said, quietly, 'would you like me to get you a drink?'

'No. No, thank you.' She gripped her hands together, her knuckles bone white. 'He…paid me a lot of attention and I…*loved* it. It was so new and exciting, and it made me feel *seen* for who I was, *needed*, not for what I did. Nobody—' she lifted her eyes to his '—had ever needed me before, in that way. I felt alive and interesting and… I… I *loved* him.' She shook her head. 'We had an affair, for a year.'

'You had an affair with a senior partner, for a year? How was that possible?'

'Oh, it had to be kept secret. That was part of the excitement of it, I suppose. We could never let anything show. But he took me to restaurants, and away for weekends. And back to his flat. Often. He travelled to New York a lot, and to the other international offices, but I was always waiting for him, when he came back to London.'

Jensen's dark eyes stayed on her face. She wished he'd look away. It felt as if he was witnessing the shame that she'd never been able to admit to anyone.

'What happened, Beth? How did it end?'

'My stepmother died, and I was free, and then I discovered I would shortly have nowhere to live. I told Charles. I genuinely believed he'd be ready to make our relationship public. I said I could resign, find another job, so it would all be okay.

We could be a proper couple. But…he looked at me as if I'd lost my mind. He said he was going back to the States, to his…*wife*. I said, "You're married?" He said, "Yes, but you're not. That's why we've been able to do this.'"

Jensen swore. 'Beth, how come you've hidden this? Why didn't you tell me? I thought we'd shared everything.'

She shook her head and gave up trying to blink back her tears. They spilled down her face and she scrubbed at them with her knuckles. 'The only person I've told is Janet. Why would I tell you?'

'Because you trust me? Or perhaps you don't.'

'Afterwards, I heard that the reason he'd returned to New York was because a case he'd prosecuted had been found to be an unsafe conviction. That was yours, of course. He didn't want to be too available, although that wouldn't stop him being investigated. He would have felt safer with the width of the Atlantic between him and possible trouble.'

'Coward.'

'Maybe.'

It was a long time before Jensen spoke again. When he did, his voice was quiet. 'Beth?'

She loved the way he said her name. It felt like a caress, even now.

'Yes?'

'Is that what you wish? That you were still

working for him, still keeping his bed warm? That I…' He swallowed and sucked in a noisy breath. 'Do you still love him, Beth?'

Her eyes closed briefly. She looked exhausted. When then they opened again they were filled with pain—the kind of pain that told him just how much she'd been hurt, how much she was still hurting.

He crossed his arms over his chest, breathing hard and fast. He'd tried to convince Beth that she needed to be free to make new choices, meet new challenges, form new friendships. An association with him would hold her back, prevent her from becoming the person she deserved to be, but she refused to accept it. She wanted to fight for their relationship.

Now he wondered if he knew her at all. How could he not have known about this hurt that she carried in her heart? He'd shared with her the pain of his failed marriage, how he'd tried his best to save it. He'd revealed how his daughter refusing to speak to him or see him had torn his heart in two.

There'd been so many opportunities for Beth to tell him how she'd been hurt, but she'd never taken any of them. Why had she waited until now? She'd once talked of a relationship she'd had when she was at college, but she'd brushed it aside, as if it had meant nothing. She'd allowed him to believe it was the only other relationship she'd had.

He could think of only one reason why she'd kept this hidden. She hadn't been open and honest with him because she didn't think he was trustworthy. Was it possible that, deep down, she did not even believe in his innocence? The feelings of inadequacy that had plagued him came crowding back, making him question whether she felt anything for him at all. Was their attraction for each other just something he'd grown to believe in because he so badly needed someone to make him feel good about himself again? Over the weeks he'd grown to believe they shared a unique connection, but he was suddenly plunged into doubt. She'd been so deeply traumatised that she couldn't bear to talk about it. She'd buried it, desperately holding onto the memories and the pain, rather than addressing them, as she'd advised him to address his own trauma. If she no longer had feelings for Charles Denby, why hadn't she been able to open her heart to him?

He'd asked her if she still loved him, and she hadn't denied it.

The chair grated on the stone terrace as he pushed it back. He stood, moving slowly, deliberately, his brain and his limbs not fully co-ordinated. He stared at Beth's tear-stained face—tears that were for the loss she'd suffered.

His wife had left him, even before his reputation had been trashed. His daughter had cancelled him from her life. The friends he'd thought were loyal had withdrawn.

Now he wondered why Beth would be any different. He'd told her he felt unworthy of her. He'd never felt more positive that he was right.

Beth's eyes still shimmered with the sheen of tears. Jensen kept his arms folded, his hands pinioned in his armpits. He would not, could not, do what his mind screamed at him to do. He would not step forward and wipe them away with the pads of his thumbs or fold her against his chest and tell her it was all okay.

It would never be okay.

He turned on his heel and began to walk towards the line of trees, to the place where the path to the beach began.

'Jensen.' Her strained, choked voice reached him and compelled him to turn round. 'How can I make you understand that I…?'

'Beth.' He said her name one last time. 'I think I understand very well.'

This time he kept walking. When he reached the safety of the sheltering trees, he broke into a run.

CHAPTER FIFTEEN

MOVING ON AUTOPILOT, her mind numb, Beth cleared away the remains of what should have been a beautiful evening. She filled a bucket with water and sluiced the spilled wine from the terrace. It had turned sticky and had already attracted a wasp. It flew up angrily, and with the small, functioning part of her brain she half wished it would sting her. At least that would be a distraction from the awful, heavy pain in her heart.

She swept up some remaining splinters of glass and pushed the salad and cold kebabs and bread into the fridge. The idea of eating made her stomach heave.

It seemed impossible to stop her eyes from straying to the gap in the trees, where the path led down to the beach, expecting to see Jensen appearing there any second. He'd have that wry, self-deprecating look on his face, be pushing a hand through his thick dark hair and apologising for being too quick to judge her.

Surely, he'd come back.

She stretched out, exhausted, on a sunbed. It was fully dark, the only light coming from the solar lamps in the garden. A lighter patch on the horizon showed where the moon would eventually rise. The day, which had started with such joy, was ending in anguish and crushed hopes. How could the tenderness Jensen had shown her this morning have turned into such angry bitterness this evening?

If she hadn't encouraged him to reconnect with the world…if she hadn't given him the Wi-Fi code…

But she couldn't allow herself to think like that. She'd done the right thing. She'd promised to fight for them both, and she'd been trying to do that.

Foolishly, she'd allowed herself to begin to imagine a future with him, instead of taking one day at a time, as she'd advised him to do. But just as the dreams she'd had as a young girl, of meeting her soulmate and falling in love, had never been allowed to come true, so was this dream destined to turn to ashes.

Much later, she retreated inside, slid the glass doors closed, and lay on the sofa, her knees pulled up and her arms wrapped around herself, and slept fitfully.

Milky dawn light woke her. The promise of sunrise lay in the band of pink and grey light along the horizon in the east, and a few bright stars still hung in the deep blue of the sky. Beth uncurled, stiff and tired, and walked out onto the terrace. The pre-dawn air was crisp and fresh but once the sun rose, she knew it would grow hot again.

Through the wakeful hours of the night, she'd rerun last night endlessly through her mind. The turn of Jensen's head, his voice speaking *that* name, the splintering of the wine bottle at her feet. Her memories were confused, blurred with shock. She'd tried to recall what she'd said. What *he'd* said.

Now, in the pearly light of dawn, she remembered something else. Jensen's voice, quiet and steady. *'Do you still love him, Beth?'*

What had she said? She struggled to remember. The question had shocked her. She'd tried to explain her feelings. But a cold certainty spread through her, making her shiver in the warm air. She hadn't answered him. Not properly. Her heart had cracked, but she'd tried to keep the feelings in. It was as if she didn't want to admit, even to herself, how she really felt about Charles Denby.

She listened for the reassuring tapping sound of *Sundance*'s rigging. Silence echoed around her. It would be a while before the cicadas began to tune up. Not a breath of breeze stirred the leaves of the trees, and she pressed her folded arms across her stomach, trying to crush the insidious coil of dread. The rigging would be silent today, the sea a sparkling kaleidoscope of blue, turquoise and green.

Her kaftan lay where she'd abandoned it yesterday afternoon, on the back of a chair, when she and Jensen had swum in the pool. She'd grown so used to wearing only her bikini that she hadn't even thought of covering up again. Now she pulled it over her head, wriggled her feet into her flip-flops and walked across the dry grass.

She had to talk to Jensen.

The light beneath the tree canopy was still dim and she trod carefully, picking her way over roots and stones. As she emerged onto the beach the sun broke free of the sea on the horizon, unfurling a path of light across the width of the bay.

Beth shaded her eyes against the sudden glare, searching the water with increasing desperation. *Sundance* had gone.

Jensen paced the deck in the dark. His habit of searching the trees for a light at the villa persisted but as always there was no sign of life up on the hillside. He drank three mugs of ferocious black coffee, laced with whisky, so at least he could blame the caffeine for the way his hands shook and his heart thumped in his chest.

The battle he fought with his body was fierce. He imagined himself climbing back into the RIB and racing back to the beach, running up the rough track. What would Beth have done, after he'd left her standing alone at the edge of the terrace? Was she sleeping in her bed—the bed he'd shared with her, where he'd held her, *loved* her?

He stopped, gripping the rail. How would she have reacted if he'd told her he loved her? Would she have admitted she was still in love with someone else? Someone who'd treated her so badly?

At the first glimmer of pale light in the east, he started *Sundance*'s engine and winched up the anchor, turning the wheel to set her on course for the narrow channel between the headlands. He tried, and failed, not to think about the last time he'd stood in the cockpit, with his hands over hers, when she'd asked him to show her how to sail. As he'd turned her in his arms her beauty and uncomplicated joy had stolen his breath and the kiss that had followed had robbed him of his heart.

He swore and opened up the engine. *Sundance* responded, gathering speed.

Once out in the open sea, he raised both sails and felt her come alive beneath his feet. He'd sail hard and hope for a freshening wind, until he found himself in that sweet spot, where the necessities of keeping *Sundance* hauled tight and cutting through the waves, perfectly trimmed and balanced, would absorb all his attention and he wouldn't be able to think of anything else.

In his pocket his forgotten phone pinged. He dug it out to turn it off, glancing at the screen.

His unwanted emails had downloaded automatically but he had no intention of reading them.

But the one at the top of the screen caught his eye. Dear Daddy...

He pressed the off switch, and the screen went black. He couldn't think about Emily now. Beth had wanted him to try to contact her, and he'd decided he would. He pushed the thought away.

He set a course that would take him east of Kekova Island, into the wide, open sea, way from the shelter of the land. The wind would be fresher there, the sailing more challenging, he thought, grimly, glancing at the sky. High cloud streamed in the distance, and he nodded. Weather was approaching, which was just what he needed.

Sailing so hard for so many hours was taxing, and being alone, he knew, it could be extremely hazardous, but Jensen pushed on, hour after hour, taking *Sundance* to her limits and keeping his mind relentlessly focussed on what he had to do to keep her there.

Cloud bubbled up in the east, climbing through the sky and eventually obscuring the sun. The wind turned gusty as it transformed from a steady blow into a gale, pushing the sea into short, steep swells capped with white foam. Some of them broke over the bow, streaming across the foredeck. *Sundance* hit a trough, juddering, and Jensen fought with the wheel to keep her on course, drenched with cold spray, but relishing being able to battle with the elements rather than his thoughts.

He knew the sensible thing to do would be to reef the sails and slow down, but he did not feel like being sensible. He wanted to push himself to the very limit.

There was a loud crack, and the vessel swung violently off course, beam-on to the breaking seas.

It was three days before Beth ventured down to the beach again.

A restless wind had sprung up the day Jensen had left, bending the treetops and curdling the sea into an opaque, choppy green. The time had passed in a blur of empty days spent swimming laps of the pool trying to tire herself out and nights spent tossing in the wide bed where they'd lain in each other's arms, but which now felt far too big for her.

The memories of Jensen, his wide shoulders and broad chest golden against the white linen, opening his arms to her, twisted in her heart like a knife. His citrussy scent lingered on the pillows and imagining the scrape of his unshaven jaw against her skin in the mornings was a bitter torment.

Every corner of the villa held a shadow of his presence, and the beach was no different. The wind had died and the bay looked empty and abandoned without the graceful shape of *Sundance* swaying gently at anchor. Memories ambushed her on the gritty sand where they'd lain, hands entwined, drying in the sun, their skin sparkling with salt crystals, and in the place in the water, overhung by rocks, where they'd made love.

There was no escape.

She followed the curved edge of the beach, where the tiny ripples of water filled her footprints behind her, and then turned and trudged towards the trees and back up the path to the villa.

The place that had been her sanctuary now seemed lonely and vaguely hostile. It no longer felt like hers and no longer felt safe. There were too many hard surfaces and sharp edges and too many echoes in the silence.

She carried her laptop to the table on the terrace and logged on to the Internet.

Jensen wasn't coming back.

He could have come back to her, but she could not go after him. What was the point of waiting any longer, hoping each day to hear the sound of *Sundance* in the bay and to see him appear through the trees? She knew that the only thing keeping her there was the possibility that he might.

She had the power to end the waiting and hoping, and she decided to use it.

She booked a flight for the following day, then

she cycled cautiously to the village to say good-
bye to Ela, and to ask Omer to arrange for someone to water the garden, and a taxi to take her
to the airport.

CHAPTER SIXTEEN

IT WAS A tall Victorian house near the river in Putney, with a blue door.

Jensen took the front steps two at a time. His suit felt a little tight and he rolled his shoulders. Perhaps he'd built muscle, sailing alone, or perhaps it was because he hadn't worn anything as restrictive as a suit for so long.

The woman who opened the door, after he'd rapped once on the brass door knocker, wore a navy linen skirt and striped top. A tall teenaged girl appeared in the passage behind her.

'Who is it, Mum?'

The woman raised her eyebrows. 'Can I help you?'

'Janet?' Jensen held out his hand. 'Janet Ayhan? I'm Jensen Heath.'

Beth stepped off the riverboat at Cadogan Pier and made her way towards the Chelsea Physic Garden, a green space on the embankment, since 1673. It was a journey she'd made twice before in the previous three weeks, and she looked forward to the sense of peace she found there. She loved imagining the ranks of apothecaries who'd trained there over the centuries, in their outdoor teaching garden.

The courses available were now limited to day-long experiences, but she'd already signed up at an adult education centre to take evening classes, which would lead to a horticultural qualification. Meanwhile, she was using her visits to this four-acre garden, which held four thousand five hundred species of medicinal, herbal and useful plants, to learn as much as possible.

It was a five-minute walk to the Embankment Gate, where she stopped for a moment between the pillars, breathing in the scent of green grass, herbs and flowers, before taking a roundabout route, which would lead her, eventually, to the pomegranate tree. It had been a surprise to find it flourishing here, in London, but she liked to look at it and hope that Omer had organised someone to water the garden at the villa and that the pomegranate she'd planted was flourishing there, too.

She moved on, past the Gardens of Edible and Useful Plants, to the seven recently restored glasshouses.

The scent of the pelargoniums was almost overpowering. She closed her eyes, brushed her fingers through the leaves, and inhaled.

Instantly, she was transported back to the heat

of a Turkish summer afternoon. She could almost hear the singing of the cicadas, feel the warmth of the sun on her skin and the cool water of the sea washing around her ankles.

Perhaps, she thought, one day she'd be able to remember all those things without the pain that accompanied them, that accompanied *her*, wherever she went.

She'd explained to Janet the reason for her abrupt return, without adding any detail about Jensen Not much had to be said between such old friends and Janet had demonstrated her sympathy in actions rather than words: the posy of flowers which her daughter—Beth's goddaughter—Myra, picked for her; the homemade biscuits in a pretty tin; a copy of one of her favourite author's latest books.

This garden was a place where she could allow herself to remember. She wanted to keep her memories safe, and here, with the scents of tropical plants surrounding her, felt like a safe place for them. One day she hoped the memories of her time in Turkey would lose the power to hurt her. She hoped they'd soften, and she'd remember the beauty and the peace, and the kindness of the people. Most of all, she hoped she'd be able to remember the wonder of falling in love with Jensen, without the pain of how he'd left her. Their time together would be something she'd cherish.

One day she'd examine the memories and be glad of them.

She allowed herself to feel faintly optimistic about the future. It was, she told herself, infinitely better than the one she'd previously imagined. She had the power to shape it, perhaps not into what she wanted, so deeply, but into something positive that would feed her creativity and give her satisfaction of a different kind. The knowledge was empowering.

She took one last, deep breath.

'Memories, Beth?'

His voice was soft, but roughened, as if clouded with deep emotion. Beth's heart lurched, then picked up an uncomfortable, fast beat. The hot rush of adrenaline raced through her, making her head spin. Her eyes flew open, and she saw the toe of a polished leather shoe behind her. She straightened and turned, looking up.

She barely recognised him. His charcoal-grey suit skimmed the wide shoulders she was used to seeing uncovered, or filling a faded tee shirt.

A white cotton shirt and pale silk tie contrasted with his deeply tanned face, his expression watchful, his dark, dark eyes uncertain. He reached out, as if to brush a strand of her hair away from her face, the gesture achingly familiar, but then his hand dropped to his side, his fingers curled into his broad palm.

She watched the movement and then her eyes

went back to his face. His thick dark and silver hair was brushed smoothly back from his forehead, strangely formal. Beth curbed the urge to reach up and ruffle it, to try to make him look more like the Jensen she knew: relaxed and slightly windswept, bare-chested in his worn board shorts.

'Jensen?'

'I'm sorry. You probably don't want me to touch you.'

'What are you doing here?' She stepped back, putting more distance between them.

Jensen pushed his hands into his pockets to stop them from reaching for her. He wanted to hold her, drink in the scent of her hair and her skin, make that shocked look disappear from her face and stop her from chewing her bottom lip. But he knew, more clearly than any of those things he wanted, that he had to try to get this right.

He'd left her, heartbroken and in tears, without giving her a chance to finish her story. He'd leapt to the conclusion that hurt him the most, because he hadn't wanted her to hurt him first. That was what he'd come to expect from life, and in his shock at her revelation he hadn't been able to believe that anything had changed.

He needed to apologise, ask for her forgiveness for the way he'd treated her. Then he would have the courage to ask the question again, even though he knew the answer might rip his heart to shreds. If she told him to leave, he would. It would be the hardest thing he'd ever have to do, but he'd listen to what she said and to what she wanted.

'How did you find me?' She sounded bewildered and shocked.

'If you still want to talk to me, after I've said what I need to say, I'll tell you.'

'What? What do you need to say? I thought you had nothing to say to me. You…left.'

'I've come to say sorry for leaving you like that. I want…*need*…to apologise for how I behaved, that night. I'm deeply sorry, for abandoning you when you were shocked and upset. I should have stayed to make sure you were all right. I should have asked…the question I asked you, again. I'm not sure you heard me the first time. You didn't answer…'

'I heard you. Jensen…'

He pulled a hand from his pocket and held it up. 'No, please let me finish. In my defence, I was shocked, too, but that is no excuse for how I behaved. The thought of you…my beautiful, tender Beth, being manipulated…'

'I was a willing victim. I said I loved the attention.'

He dropped his head and pressed his fingers to his forehead. 'Is there somewhere else we can talk?' Other visitors had entered the glasshouse, chatting loudly. 'That is, if you want to talk to me.'

Beth indicated the door behind him. 'I'm not sure that I do. I appreciate your apology, but if that is what you came to say, I think we're done.'

Panic fluttered somewhere behind his breastbone. There'd been time for her to reflect on their relationship and maybe she'd decided she didn't need him in her life. He'd told her that, often enough. If she sent him away he'd go, but he'd come back, fighting. He looked over his shoulder. 'There's a café. I saw it on my way here. Would you like a cup of tea?'

He watched the hesitation simmer in her eyes, but then she nodded. 'All right. If you have more to say it'll be easier over tea.' She pushed past him and led the way to the door.

The cup rattled against the saucer as Beth put it down. The café was busy, but Jensen had found a table in the corner, at the edge of the paved area. She still felt a little shaky after the shock of his sudden appearance. His apology had been sincere, she was sure, and a week ago, she thought, she would have rushed into his arms, but recently she'd felt some of her strength, fought for and built up during her time in Turkey, returning. The memories of Jensen were painful, but at least she'd been able to examine them. And rather than blaming herself for the way he'd left, she questioned his abrupt departure.

She'd been distraught, her ankle cut by flying glass, and he'd walked away. Not only had he walked away, he'd sailed away, and he hadn't come back to check that she was okay.

'Thank you for the tea. What else was it you wanted to say?' She glanced at her watch.

'Are you in a hurry? What time does the garden close?'

'Five o'clock but I want to catch the next boat back to Putney.'

She watched him pick up a spoon and turn it over in his fingers. The memories of the exquisite sensations those long, strong fingers could provoke in her made her shiver involuntarily, and she looked away.

'Beth,' he said, replacing the spoon beside his cup, and capturing her eyes in his direct gaze, 'I've apologised for how I behaved the night I left you. Whatever becomes of us, however you feel about me, I will regret that for ever. I'm truly sorry.'

She nodded. 'It was…horrible. I waited for you to come back. And the next morning, I found you'd sailed away.'

'It was thoughtless and unkind. But I'd asked you a question, and you hadn't answered me. I was afraid that, if you did, I wouldn't like the answer. I ran, again.'

'You must understand now that I know what running away feels like, especially from something that is not your fault.'

He nodded. 'Yes. I do. It is not the solution.'

'No, it's not, but it's not easy to get to that understanding, either. When I remember how I was when I first arrived at the villa, and look at myself now, even after you'd left me, I feel like a different person.'

'How?'

'I'm strong, Jensen. I was strong in my job. I was known to be determined, iron-willed and inflexible. But inflexibility snaps easily. There's greater strength in being flexible. You're more likely to bounce back up if you're knocked down.'

'Is that what you've done?'

'No, but I think I might be able to. One day.' She bent to pick up her bag, keeping her head down, not wanting him to see how difficult this was for her to say.

'Beth, before you go, I need to know the answer.'

She raised her head and stared at him. 'I was shocked by your question, Jensen. I couldn't believe you'd need to ask it, after everything we'd shared. If you could believe that of me, I thought perhaps I didn't know you at all. But the answer is no, I do not still love him.' She stood up, needing to escape before she cried. 'In fact, I know now that I never loved him at all. Being with you taught me that.'

He watched her walk away, her back straight, her head high, her lovely hair blowing around her shoulders, and he remembered her saying she was going to fight for them both.

She wouldn't need to now. He would be doing the fighting.

He had to queue to pay for their tea. He couldn't go after her. It was the longest wait of his life, or so it felt. She'd vanished by the time he came out of the café and he had no idea which way she'd gone. Whichever way was the way to the river, he thought, desperately, looking for signposts.

He was the last person to board the boat. He'd run, and decided he wasn't as fit as he could be, as he bent to put his hands on his knees and catch his breath. When he straightened, he couldn't see her anywhere. Had this been a mad, pointless idea, to follow her and try again? He'd promised he'd do what she wanted, but she hadn't actually asked him to go away, had she?

He threaded his way through the covered section, searching for a glimpse of that bright hair or that emerald-green cardigan. It was cool on the river. Surely she'd have chosen a seat inside?

But she wasn't there. His heart, still beating painfully fast after his dash along the embankment, refused to slow down, even though he'd got his ragged breathing under better control. He pushed through the doors onto the open rear section of the boat. It was deserted.

Then suddenly, there she was, tucked into a corner against the rail, out of the wind, looking out across the river, with her sunglasses on and her hair blowing behind her. His heart lurched, remembering her on *Sundance*, loving the experience of sailing, challenging herself to try new things, her example challenging *him* to become a stronger, better person.

She turned, evidently sensing his presence behind her. 'Jensen? You followed me.'

He frowned down at her. 'I ran,' he said, 'but this time it wasn't away from something which scared me. It was towards you. Please, Beth, will you give me another chance?'

Her green eyes studied him for what felt like much too long. Then she reached up and ruffled his hair. 'There,' she said. 'Now you look more like yourself.'

He smiled in relief, daring to slip an arm around her shoulders. 'And you simply look more beautiful than ever.'

They left the boat at Putney. Beth stood on the embankment, clutching her shoulder bag.

'It's a ten-minute walk from here, along the river. How did you get here?'

'My car is parked near Janet's house, if it hasn't been towed away by now. Janet suggested looking for you at the garden.'

'You can walk with me, then. It's this way.'

They walked in silence, their shoulders bumping against one another. They'd hardly spoken on the boat, either, spending what was left of the journey standing, with Jensen's arm around her shoulders. It had felt strange, out of context, but also achingly familiar.

Outside the house, Beth turned to him. 'You haven't told me how you found me,' she said.

'Yes, I did. Janet suggested I try the garden.'

'That's not what I meant. How did you find your way to Janet?'

'That story is too long to tell on a doorstep. Will you come out for the day with me tomorrow?'

This felt like a parting of ways. In one direction lay the safe path. In the other, a path that led somewhere unknown and challenging, possibly rough in places. She knew what she should choose.

'Yes, please,' she said, letting go of the safe Beth, the Beth everyone knew. Only Jensen knew the other version of her.

CHAPTER SEVENTEEN

THEY HAD A picnic on Parliament Hill, sitting on a rug with the city spread out below, the Thames a thread of silver winding through its midst. They walked on Hampstead Heath, occasionally linking hands, talking about their time together in Turkey.

They dashed back to Jensen's car when sudden rainclouds threatened to drench them. Jensen turned to her, seeing the bloom of colour in her cheeks, which had been missing the day before, and the smile he'd longed for.

'Let me show you my apartment. This rain looks set.' He peered through the windscreen at the downpour. 'But if it lets up you can see my roof terrace, too. I could do with some advice on what to grow. It was neglected while I was in prison.'

Beth nodded her agreement, noticing the new ease with which he referred to the time he'd been imprisoned. It had been an awful time for him, but the bitterness with which he usually spoke of it had faded.

Now, she stood looking out at the futuristic landscape of the City of London, the Thames wide and grey many floors below, the gleaming dome of St Paul's Cathedral visible between the soaring, thrusting skyscrapers. She heard the soft pop of a cork being extracted from a bottle, and then Jensen handed her a glass of wine.

'Thank you.' She sat at the end of the enormous sofa, which faced the view, while Jensen occupied an armchair opposite. Awareness had been building between them all day, every touch of a hand or smiling glance increasing the tension. She was pleased he'd chosen to sit a distance away from her. She wanted to listen to what he had to say without the distraction of his physical closeness.

'I said I'd tell you how I found you.'

'What happened, Jensen? I really need to know.'

'Before I start, I have something for you.' He lifted a package from the table and handed it to her. 'You forgot to pack this when you left.'

Beth pulled one of her pink flip-flops from the wrapping.

'What?' He smiled at her incredulity. 'How…?' She turned it over in her hands. It still smelled of salt and the sea. 'I couldn't find it when I left.' Her hands stilled and her eyes widened as realisation dawned. 'You went back, Jensen. You went back to find me.'

* * *

'I sailed hard. Too hard, as it turned out.' Jensen put his glass on the coffee table between them. 'I was half out of my mind with despair and anger and all I could think of doing was pushing *Sundance* to the limit so that anything else would be pushed out of my brain. I went east of Kekova Island, because I knew the wind would be stronger on the open sea. It was, and it picked up all afternoon. I was tired—I'd hardly slept.'

'I hardly slept, either. I went down to the beach as soon as it grew light. I was desperate to talk to you…'

'I'm so sorry, Beth. I… I just felt bitter and angry. In my shock, I thought that because you hadn't denied it, you still loved him. I thought it was no less than I should have expected. Nothing much had gone right in my life for a while, apart from you, and a part of me wanted to protect myself by leaving you before you could leave me.'

'What happened? Is *Sundance*…?'

'*Sundance* is fine. But she's not a new boat and I asked too much of her. The backstay broke, leaving us in danger of losing the main mast, in a heavy sea. I dropped the sails and tried to rig up a temporary repair but sailing on your own there's not a lot you can do, safely. I started the engine and that was when I realised I'd made another, very basic error. I had very little fuel. I'd planned to get more but…like I said, I wasn't thinking straight. I tried to conserve the fuel by sailing under the mizen sail, but I couldn't make much headway in such a heavy sea. Early the next morning a fishing boat spotted us. The storm had blown over, but the swells were still big, and *Sundance* was being steadily washed towards a rocky shore, which would not have been…it wouldn't have ended well. They towed us to a sheltered anchorage and left us there. They picked us up again on their return journey, two days later, and took us around to the leeward side of the island, to a small marina on an isolated peninsular of the mainland. It was safe, but I knew it would take days to get *Sundance* repaired.'

'Is that where she is now?'

He nodded. 'She's perfectly safe, but I'll have to get the right fittings shipped out and have help repairing the damage.'

'Okay. That's good, but it must have been scary…'

'It was, and I only really appreciated how close we'd come to disaster once we were safe. But it was good, too.'

'*How?*'

'I was shaken, and very tired, but after having something to eat and catching up on sleep I had time to think. Lots of time. And I remembered, very clearly, something we'd talked about.'

'What?'

'About the ruined city. How people must have

been going about their lives, when suddenly, in a flash, everything changed for ever. How you never know what tomorrow, or even today, might bring, and it's important to live every moment in the best way you can because things we take for granted in life can be snatched away in a moment. It's rare to get second chances, when things go wrong, but that's what I've had, and you, too. And us.'

'Jensen…'

'Let me finish. Please.' He swallowed a mouthful of wine. 'I've spent the past year believing I'd lost everything; that my life was wrecked; that nothing I could do would bring it back. But I've been exonerated and now I have the chance to start again and build a life, which I hope will be better than the old one.'

Beth nodded. 'That's a positive step to take.'

'I'd lost the foundations on which I'd built my life and, waiting for that fishing boat to come back for me, I realised I was afraid that I'd lost you, too. I walked away because I was afraid of what you were going to say. I thought about how I'd known I loved you and I'd never told you. We always think there'll be the chance to do the things we want or plan, but sometimes that chance doesn't happen. Suddenly, with desperate clarity, I knew I didn't want that to happen to us, and I knew I had to get back to you, at least to tell you my true feelings.'

'Jensen...'

'Shh. The place where I left *Sundance* is only accessible by boat. I thought about trying to make a temporary repair to the backstay, but decided I'd already been foolish enough. Luckily the RIB had survived the drama without being washed off the platform at the stern, so I set off in that. The wind had dropped, and it was calm but it still took hours and hours. I had to stop once at a small harbour to refuel.'

'Did you stop at Sula? Omer and Ela knew I'd left.'

'No. I kept going. I was desperate to get back to you. But when I got to the villa I knew at once you'd gone. It was locked up and deserted. The only trace of you I found was your flip-flop. I motored back down the coast to Sula and Omer told me you'd left that morning.'

'I'd waited for you for three days and then I couldn't bear to wait any longer. I had to make something happen, so I left.'

'I was panic-stricken. I thought there was no way I could find you. Because I'd been so stubborn about using my phone, we'd never swapped contact details. Returning to *Sundance* and making her secure took the best part of a week, and then I managed to get a taxi to the airport at Antalya and a flight back to London.'

'You must have been exhausted.'

'I was. The whole experience taught me that

my solo sailing days are over. I won't be doing that again.'

'I'm glad. My journey home wasn't exciting at all. Just sad. I've been staying with Janet, again, but I'm looking at a small flat tomorrow. And I have a job interview, at a nursery garden, next week.'

'I thought you'd be with Janet, at least at first.'

'But you haven't told me how you found *her*. Last night, she wouldn't tell me, either. I think she wanted to make sure that I didn't change my mind about today.'

'Once I sat down to think, logically, I remembered that you'd said Janet's husband was Omer's cousin.'

'Ahh. It's starting to become clear.'

'I went to find him and he gave me their address in Putney. Janet didn't know where you'd gone yesterday, but she said I should try the Physic Garden. She said it's your favourite place.'

Beth nodded. 'In London, yes, it is. She and Myra were excited to meet you yesterday.'

'I was torn when I got back. Part of me wanted to find you immediately, but I thought perhaps you needed time...' He stood up and paced to the window. 'It was torture, knowing you were here, but waiting, and not knowing if I was doing the right thing.' He came around the coffee table and sat on the sofa, leaving space between them.

'Also, there were a couple of things I wanted to do first.'

'Have you seen James?'

'I have. That was one of them.'

'Did you tell him where you've been? Explain your silence?'

'Yes. He'd guessed I'd have headed off somewhere on *Sundance*. He understood my silence, especially when I told him *something* about what I'd been doing...'

'*Jensen.*' A faint flush crept up over her cheeks.

'When he meets you, he'll understand even better.'

'You have plans for us to meet?'

'Not just James. There's someone else I'd like you to meet if you want.'

Beth's brows drew together. 'Who?'

'When I logged onto your villa's Wi-Fi my emails downloaded. I decided I should read them while waiting to be rescued. Well, one of them, anyway. It was from Emily.'

'Your daughter?' The delight in her voice was obvious.

'Yes. She wanted to see me.'

'Oh, Jensen, I'm so pleased.'

'She'd like to meet you.'

'You *told* her about me?'

'I told her I'd met someone very important and special, but I'd screwed up, big time. I said I needed to find you to fix it.'

'What did she say?'

'She rolled her eyes and said, "Typical." And then she said, "Go and find her, Dad." So I did.'

'That's the best news I've heard in just about for ever, Jensen.' Beth blinked back tears. 'I'm so, so happy for you both.'

'Beth, sweetheart, don't cry.' He reached for her, and she felt herself pulled towards him.

'They're happy tears.'

But he didn't let her go. She felt the solidity of his body against hers, breathed in the scent of him, which she'd last inhaled on his pillow in the villa, trying to keep his memory whole. He skimmed the tears away from her cheeks with his thumbs and his big, weather-roughened hands framed her face. 'Can you ever forgive me for hurting you?'

'You said once you couldn't regret what had happened to you, because without it you wouldn't have met me. Do you remember?'

He nodded. 'Yes, I do remember. I also remember the sense of wonder I felt at the realisation, because it was so utterly true.'

'After you left me, the one thought I had was that, however sad it made me, I would never, ever regret what we'd had together. And I don't.'

His arms encircled her, and she felt infinitely safe. One broad hand splayed across the small of her back and the other drifted up her spine to cup the back of her head, tipping her face up towards his. His fingers tangled in her hair and she felt his breath ghost across the top of her head.

'May I kiss you?'

'Mmm.'

Jensen's arm curved round Beth's shoulders, pulling her against his side, his other hand smoothing her hair behind her ear and then resting on the place above the tip of her collarbone where he could feel her pulse fluttering. Her breathing was still quick.

'Hey.'

'Mmm.'

'I didn't mean that to happen. I was going to open a bottle of wine and show you the view, sit and talk and then take you out for dinner, properly, on a date.'

'The view from here is quite good.' She glanced up at him, and her smile did something strange to his heart. 'Not sure the London skyline can compete.'

He laughed softly and kissed the top of her head. 'You still have a tan.'

He brushed his lips over her mouth and rested his forehead against hers. 'Please, Beth, will you agree to stay with me? Be my soulmate? I love you more than I'll ever be able to express in words.'

He knew by her smile that her tears were still happy ones.

'When you turned up on my beach—' she slanted a look at him through her lashes '—all we each wanted was to be alone, but fate had other plans for us. Being loved by you is the best, most amazing thing that has ever happened to me, and all the love I have, which nobody else has ever needed, I want to give to you.' She stroked a hand across his chest. He captured it in his, turning it over and kissing her palm.

'Thank you. In the midst of thinking I'd lost everything, I found you, and you are all I need. You *are* everything to me.'

EPILOGUE

BETH'S AIRCRAFT CIRCLED over the glittering sea before making its final approach to land at Antalya.

She spotted Jensen in the crowded concourse quickly. He looked faintly anxious, his dark eyes scanning the faces of the passengers who streamed through the glass doors from the arrivals hall. His spontaneous wide smile, when he saw her, sent warmth and pleasure racing through her.

His arms were strong and tight around her, his kiss firm. 'I'm so pleased you're here.'

'Did you think I might change my mind?'

'No, but… I just don't like being apart from you.' He took her cabin bag, keeping a protective arm around her. 'Let's go. *Sundance* is as good as new.'

Beth had been hesitant at first, when Jensen had suggested she return to Turkey and sail *Sundance* back to Greece with him. But he'd spread a map out on his dining table and described, gently, how they could island-hop all the way, sailing during the day and stopping at an island each evening.

If the weather was poor, they could afford to wait a few days. There was no rush.

'We'll be back in good time for you to start the horticulture course and by then you might have heard from the Physic Garden about the volunteering job.'

'I'm really looking forward to studying again. Being able to do something I've wanted almost all my life feels like a gift.'

'That's what you are to me.' He'd pulled her against him. 'A very rare and precious gift. I still can't believe I have you in my life. And I've had positive feedback about the programme I'm planning to set up. Apparently, mentoring prisoners to prepare them for life back in the community is massively under-resourced and I'll be able to make a real difference. That's all I want to do—help people less fortunate and less able to help themselves.'

Jensen held Beth's hand as she stepped from the pontoon onto *Sundance*'s deck. 'Welcome back aboard. We've been waiting for this day. She's fit to sail again. We'll take her out for a trial this afternoon. But I'll be treating her gently from now on.'

Beth put her arms around his waist. 'As gently as you treat me?'

He dropped a kiss onto her mouth. 'If that's what you want. Sometimes I'm not so sure.'

She laughed. 'Perhaps I'll schedule some trial time, too.'

'No need to schedule it. We've all the time we need. Well, four weeks, and that's more than enough time to sail back to the marina in Piraeus in a sedate and leisurely way.'

'I'm not sure about sedate…'

'No, nor am I. There was not much that was sedate about you the night before I left.'

'Speak for yourself, Jensen. I was expecting a lie-in the next morning.'

'And that's what you had. A lie-in, with me.'

'I did.' Beth yawned. 'Not this morning, though. I had to get up insanely early to catch the flight. I think I need a siesta.'

'I also had to get up early to meet you. The sea trials can wait until tomorrow. I've booked a restaurant for this evening.'

They sat in *Sundance*'s cockpit later, after dinner, watching the last of the daylight drain from the sky and the sea turn from deep blue to burnished pewter. Jensen pulled Beth tightly against his side. He hadn't expected to feel nervous, but his voice shook slightly.

'I want to do this properly, Beth.' He took a deep breath. 'I love you with all my heart and soul. Please will you marry me?'

Her green eyes flew wide and he loved that he'd been able to take her by surprise.

'Oh, Jensen, of course I will.' Then she gasped as he took a small box from his pocket and eased the velvet-covered lid open. 'Oh, it's the most exquisite ring.'

He slipped it onto her finger and turned her in his arms to kiss her. 'I wanted to surprise you. Have I?'

Beth put a hand up to his cheek and the solitaire diamond shone in the soft twilight. 'It's the best surprise I've ever had. I love you, so much. Thank you for loving me. This is the perfect way to start our journey into the future together.'

'As long as we're together, whatever we do will be an adventure. And our love will grow stronger, with each one.'

His kiss was warm and demanding, her response urgent.

'Yes,' she whispered, 'starting now.'

* * * * *

If you enjoyed this story,
check out these other great reads
from Suzanne Merchant

Heiress's Escape to South Africa
Ballerina and the Greek Billionaire
Off-Limits Fling with the Billionaire
Their Wildest Safari Dream

All available now!